'That's blackmail.'

Claudia gaped at Morgan. He must be insane.

'Morgan,' she purred, 'haven't you got this completely the wrong way round? You have far more reason to fear the truth coming out than I do. *I'm* the one who could blackmail *you!*'

'You could, Claudia, but would you?'

She lowered her dark lashes as if thinking, her eyes shot with gold as she studied his impassive face.

'I dare you!' he said softly.

Dear Reader

In February, we celebrate one of the most romantic times of the year—St Valentine's Day, when messages of true love are exchanged. At Mills & Boon we feel that our novels carry the Valentine spirit on throughout the year and we hope that readers agree. Dipping into the pages of our books will give you a taste of true romance every month...so chase away those winter blues and look forward to spring with Mills & Boon!

Till next month,

The Editor

Susan Napier was born on St Valentine's Day, so it's not surprising she has developed an enduring love of romantic stories. She started her writing career as a journalist in Auckland, New Zealand, trying her hand at romantic fiction only after she had married her handsome boss! Numerous books later she still lives with her most enduring hero, two future heroes—her sons!—two cats and a computer. When she's not writing she likes to read and cook, often simultaneously!

Recent titles by the same author:

THE HAWK AND THE LAMB

THE CRUELLEST LIE

BY

SUSAN NAPIER

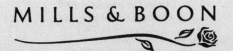

MILLS & BOON

MILLS & BOON LIMITED
ETON HOUSE, 18-24 PARADISE ROAD
RICHMOND, SURREY TW9 1SR

For Liz Pollack
The Parkroyal Hotel, Wellington

*First published in Great Britain 1993
by Mills & Boon Limited*

© Susan Napier 1993

*Australian copyright 1993
Philippine copyright 1994
This edition 1994*

ISBN 0 263 78390 1

*Set in Times Roman 10 on 11 pt.
01-9402-60075 C*

Made and printed in Great Britain

CHAPTER ONE

'The cruellest lies are often told in silence.'
Robert Louis Stevenson

'YOU'RE pregnant!'

Claudia, who had found precious little reason to laugh over the past few months, looked down at the small mound under her flimsy, faded cotton sundress and felt a thrill of amusement lift her embattled spirts.

'My goodness, so I am!' she declared in tones of mock-horrified discovery to the black-browed stranger frowning at her from her doorstep. 'And to think of all that money I've been wasting on Weight Watchers!'

Instead of amusing him, her flippancy deepened the frown, the man's crooked, surly mouth tightening ominously. He was tall—quite startlingly so—and correspondingly lean, with close-cropped midnight-black hair contrasting with surprisingly pale skin and a shadow on his jutting jaw that added to the general aura of menace radiating from eyes grimly slitted against the afternoon sun. In fact, if it weren't for his achingly elegant grey suit and a discreet silk tie that whispered of extravagant wealth and excellent taste, Claudia might have been afraid. As it was she assumed that he must have knocked on the wrong door.

'Very funny.' Perversely, his acid reply made Claudia even more amused.

'Thank you, I thought so, too. Do you usually start conversations with total strangers by stating the obvious?'

'If anyone's being obvious here, it's you... *Very* obvious.' The clipped pronouncement of distaste and pointed reference to her swollen abdomen tempered her amusement with annoyance. He was obviously too stuffy to appreciate her teasing. On the other hand nobody liked being laughed at for an honest mistake and it wasn't really fair of her to play on his ignorance, but she couldn't resist one more dig.

She sighed loudly. 'OK, I'll bite. What are you selling? Vaccum cleaners? Encylopaedias?' She gave him the cynical once-over of a typically harassed housewife, knowing that he couldn't possibly be a salesman, let alone one of the door-to-door variety. For one thing he was clearly lacking in the main essential—ingratiating charm.

Sure enough he stiffened at the very suggestion.

'I'm not selling anything.'

'Not to me, at any rate,' she agreed. 'First day on the job, huh? You really must do something about that technique of yours if you expect to make a living door-to-door...'

'I am *not* a salesman!' The crisp consonants vibrated dangerously against the growling vowels and Claudia decided that she was in danger of letting her unaccustomed frivolity run away with her. Now was the time to smooth the savagely ruffled male ego with some of her famous tact.

'Of course you're not——' she began soothingly, only to be cut off by his furious hiss.

'Don't patronise me—*Miss* Lawson!'

The emphasis on her single status, as well as the realisation that he knew her identity, was like a dash of icy water in her face, washing away the dregs of humour and clarifying the reasons for his accusing contempt.

Claudia felt a dreary, dispiriting, and totally unreasonable disappointment in her unexpected visitor. She had faced narrow-minded prejudice often enough lately to recognise its stony façade. The half-smile which had softened the pinched lines of her narrow face congealed into a grim line. She suddenly felt exposed by the harsh light of the hot summer's day, and hated him for making her aware of her terrible vulnerability.

Was he a reporter? No, no more than he was a salesman. Newspapers didn't pay their journalists enough to afford thousand-dollar suits.

'Then get to the point, Mr...?' She lifted her eyebrows in a gesture that she knew emphasised the natural haughtiness of her delicate features. Chris had called her beautiful and, even though she thought that her face was too sharp for conventional prettiness, he had made her believe it. These days it was even sharper, refined by the nausea that constantly blighted her appetite and the sheer strain of putting on a brave, unconcerned face for the world.

He ignored her implicit command. 'Is Mark in?'

'Mark?' As she had been expecting another oblique attack on her morals, his innocent query about her boarder took her off-guard.

'Mark Stone.'

'Mark Stone.' She repeated the name slowly to give herself time to think. Innocent? This man? Definitely not. Was he ferreting for information about her or about Mark? Was *he* the reason that the young man had been acting oddly guilty in the past few weeks? Had Mark got into some kind of trouble and not wanted to add to Claudia's burdens by worrying her with his personal problems?

Claudia looked again at her visitor, who was waiting with unconcealed impatience for her reply. Overt evidence of wealth was no guarantee of honesty and integrity, as she had very good reason to know. On second glance the slickly formal clothing didn't disguise the threat of that crookedly sneering mouth, the coldly narrowed eyes or the tension in the muscles of his neck and the set of his shoulders under the slim-fitting jacket. He had come expecting trouble and was prepared to handle it aggressively. Ruthless was the descriptive epithet that sprang to mind.

Was he a con man, or some kind of heavy, come to collect on an outstanding debt? Her eyes flicked past the scowling stranger to the car parked outside the gate of her small suburban home. A silver Jaguar as coldly sophisticated and sleekly solid as the man in front of her.

She made her decision. 'He's not here,' she said bluntly.

Not surprisingly, he didn't make a gracious expression of regret and politely leave.

'I know he lives here.' His grating statement challenged her to deny it.

'Well, I'm sorry, he's not at home,' she replied, not trying to hide her satisfaction at thwarting him.

'Really?' Neither did he try to hide his disbelief. 'Not at home, or just not at home to *me*?'

'Since I don't know who you are I guess it's both,' she said crisply.

'I'll wait.'

'You do that.' Little gold flecks of malice shimmered in her caramel-brown eyes. She hoped he would roast in his stuffy suit waiting for a victim who would never arrive, though no doubt his expensive car had air-conditioning.

'Thank you.' Before she realised what he was doing he had whipped past her with an agility astonishing in someone so tall, and was striding down the cool hall, looking into the rooms on either side.

'Hey! What do you think you're doing?'

She had left all the internal doors in the house open to help circulate the turgid summer air and by the time she had caught up with her uninvited guest he had swiftly inspected the empty kitchen and bathroom and the two bedrooms, one of which contained a double bed, the other a divan and a partly assembled rocking cradle along with a desk and chair.

Knowing that there was no way she could stop him by force, Claudia stormed into the compact, L-shaped living-room ahead of him. Energy boiled inside her, banishing the weary lethargy that had been a constant companion to her pregnancy.

'As you can see, Mark isn't here!' she reiterated sarcastically. 'Perhaps you'd like to check the cupboards and pull up the carpets in case he's hiding in the cellar!'

'Do you have a cellar?'

Claudia blinked at his hard suspicion. Was the man utterly devoid of any sense of humour or proportion?

'No!' she bit out. 'I wish I did. It would be somewhere to lock you until the men in white coats come and fetch you!'

'You think I'm mad? You haven't seen anything yet, Miss Lawson.' So he *could* smile, but it was no consolation. In fact, the crooked quirk of his lips was most unnerving. There was no softening of humour in it and certainly no intention to amuse. Even more unnerving were his eyes. Now they were no longer squinted against the sun she could see that they were a gorgeous, breathtakingly intense blue. The blunt features and hard jaw were almost unattractive in their ruggedness, but those eyes were almost hypnotic in their vivid splendour.

'Where is he?'

With difficulty she tore her gaze away from his drilling stare. 'Why should I tell you?'

'Because I ask?'

She almost laughed. 'You call this *asking*? I call it arrogant bullying and invasion of privacy.'

'I didn't know you had any privacy left to invade, *Miss* Lawson.' Again that cynically contemptuous emphasis, accompanied by the piercing stare. 'The way you

and your famous lover cavorted for the Press I doubt
that you even know what the word means.'

Claudia wished that she could icily refute his sneer
but the truth was that Chris *had* revelled in the fame
that his race-driving career had brought him. Loving and
being loved by him had meant embracing his fame,
sharing a large chunk of their relationship with his devoted public, accepting her place in the limelight beside
him, if not whole-heartedly then at least with dignity
and grace.

In the first few months after he was killed in a race-
track crash the publicity had been even more intrusive
and wildly speculative but Claudia had simply withdrawn, and her resolute refusal to feed the old gossip or
provide any fuel for the new had led to her present
blissful anonymity. But she would not allow this narrow-
minded bigot to belittle what she and Chris had shared
just because he believed what he read in the scandal
rags...

'Thank you for that illuminating insight into your
petrified morality——'

'On the contrary,' he cut her off sharply. 'I have a
very modern flexibility on the subject of morality. For
instance I don't subscribe to the old-fashioned notion
that a child is condemned by illegitimacy. If you think
that my son is going to marry you just because you've
cleverly managed to get yourself pregnant you have
another think coming!'

A light as dazzling as his vivid eyes switched on in her
brain. Of course! The black hair, the lean physique, the
deep crushed-velvet voice! Only there the resemblance
ended. Mark's eyes might only be a motley hazel but
otherwise his face had a male-model perfection that he
had not inherited from his father. It was no wonder that
she hadn't guessed straight away. Somehow Mark had
given her the impression that his father was much older,
but this man looked barely forty. And no wonder he had

looked so shocked by her pregnancy when she had opened the door! She almost grinned. This time she knew for certain that he had made a mistake. But in view of his anger she didn't think that he'd find it any more amusing than he had their misunderstanding on the doorstep.

'If I thought your son wanted to marry me, I'd run screaming in the other direction, Mr Stone,' she said drily and with perfect truth. 'It *is* Mr Stone, isn't it?'

'You know damned well it is,' he snarled.

'Oh, and how would I know that? As I recall you didn't bother to introduce yourself before you barged in.' From what she had gleaned from Mark, such arrogance was par for the course for Morgan Stone.

Mark had told her very little about his background other than that he was from Wellington, and that his mother had died when he was young, leaving him to be brought up by a wealthy, autocratic, perfectionist father whose expectations of his only child and heir were increasingly rigid and unrealistic. A business student at Auckland University, Mark had had a final blow-up with his father six months ago and had broken off all contact. Confronting the powerful image of his father in the flesh, Claudia could sympathise with Mark's desperate need to assert himself by proving he could make it by himself.

'If tests confirm that your child is Mark's I'll naturally arrange financial support during your pregnancy,' Morgan Stone continued coldly. 'If you wish to bring up the child yourself I'll establish a trust fund. My lawyer, as trustee, will approve expenditure strictly in the interest of the child so don't expect to be able to live the high life on my account. If you don't want to be bothered with the baby I'll make the appropriate arrangements——'

A chill of unnamed fear shuddered down Claudia's spine. She placed both hands over her swollen stomach and fought to control a sudden surge of nausea at what she thought he was implying, appalled by his cold-blooded recital and suddenly deeply aware of her physical fragility. She knew that she was unusually small—her doctor was constantly urging her to put on more weight—but she had seemed to do so only at the expense of the rest of her body so that while her bosom and stomach had continued to slowly bloom the rest of her had seemed to shrink, her face and arms and legs losing their formerly rounded contours. She might not look the picture of blooming motherhood but she wanted this child, she *needed* it...

'If you're suggesting an abortion,' she said raggedly, 'you can forget it. It's too late. This is *my* baby. It's nothing to do with you——'

'If it's my grandchild, it has everything to do with me,' he countered grimly. 'And my moral flexibility doesn't happen to include accepting abortion as a belated form of contraception, especially for a woman as sexually experienced as yourself. I meant only that I would take custody of my grandchild, if you proved unwilling or incapable of providing a secure home...' His fathomless blue eyes moved down her body as he spoke, studying her with blatantly hostile curiosity. Was he wondering what his son saw in her?

The dress Claudia wore was very thin, the humid Auckland summer heat being as taxing to her slim reserves of strength as was her nausea. This morning she had uninterestedly pulled on the coolest thing to hand, which was not actually a maternity dress at all. The spearing glance made her acutely aware of the feminine ripeness of her body, the way the flimsy bodice strained across her breasts, barely containing their lush bounty, the tautness of the fabric across her burgeoning stomach. There was nothing leering in the look and yet Claudia could feel herself flushing wildly. The placid maternal acceptance of the radical changes taking place within her body was momentarily swamped by the sensual realisation that, like the crude stone carvings of a primitive bygone era, she was to male eyes a brazen symbol of fertility, of voluptuous female sexuality. When this man looked at her, it was with the sure knowledge of her intimate experience.

A strange shock quivered along her bones. This hard, virile man a *grandfather*? Grandfather to *her* child? The first idea was almost laughable, the second utterly repugnant.

He took a step towards her and she gasped and lurched backwards, almost falling when the arm of a chair caught the back of her knees. Only his hands locking on her thickened waist saved her. She instinctively grabbed at his powerful wrists and tried to wrench them free.

'L-let me go.'

'What did you think I was going to do, hit you?' he growled roughly. 'I don't hit women—let alone women in your condition. You went very pale for a moment there; I thought you were going to faint. You'd better sit down.'

'I don't——' Even as she protested he was pushing her back into the chair, holding her there in spite of her squirming. He was not only strong, he was also extremely stubborn.

'You blanch at the idea of an abortion and yet you seem to have no problem with the concept of starving your baby in the womb,' he told her tersely. 'I suppose you're too worried about losing your figure to eat a properly balanced diet. What are you—about four or five months along? Yet you barely weigh anything and your arms are like twigs.' He bent to demonstrate his blistering point by wrapping his hand around her upper arm, his fingers overlapping on her smooth flesh.

'I'm naturally small-boned,' said Claudia defensively, loath to go into the dreary details of her difficult pregnancy with this unfeeling man. She was going to enjoy immensely seeing him eat crow when she told him the truth. 'Now will you please remove your hand? I don't like being mauled by ham-fisted male chauvinists. You know nothing about my pregnancy——' She twisted her body and he let her go, straightening to loom over her.

'I know that there are risks a woman of your age having her first baby should take care to avoid——'

'A woman *my* age!' Claudia's intention of boldly slapping him with the truth was ambushed by outrage. 'What has my age got to do with it? I'm only twenty-four!'

'A good six years older than Mark,' he took the opportunity to point out smoothly.

'I know how old he is!' Claudia gritted. When she had offered room and board to a university student she had been thinking in terms of a girl but when an eighteen-year-old Greek god had turned up on her doorstep six months ago with his wistful tale of family rejection she had let him talk his way into her life. She had never regretted the decision. His cheerfulness and fierce energy and optimism had rescued her from the dangerous inertia of grief into which she had been sliding.

'But I'm surprised *you* do,' she added tartly. 'You didn't even send him a card on his birthday.'

Mark had told her he hadn't expected any softening from his father, but she had seen the veiled disappointment in his eyes when the minor rite of passage had passed unacknowledged by his family.

'Because he didn't see fit to inform me of his whereabouts at the time, and no doubt you wouldn't have urged him to make contact. Not before you had him well and truly hooked——'

'Don't be ridiculous!' Claudia tilted her head to glare up at him, struggling to retain her dignity in her inferior position. She was glad that the heat had prompted her to twist her waterfall of straight black hair into a topknot instead of leaving it to brush her shoulders casually as she usually did. It gave her a much needed air of sophistication that might go a little way towards counteracting her the rest of her dishevelled appearance. Thanks to her swollen ankles she wasn't even wearing *shoes*, for goodness' sake!

'Mark is a responsible, intelligent young man——'

'With the emphasis on *young*——'

'Who is quite capable—insistent, in fact—of making his own decisions. Perhaps if *you* had been more receptive to his feelings he wouldn't have——'

'Run off the rails into your eager arms?'

'Will you *stop* putting words in my mouth?' Claudia rose defiantly, albeit with a little difficulty, to her feet again. 'Mr Stone, if this is the way you conduct your personal affairs I'm not surprised that you're having difficulties——'

'And you, of course, are famous for conducting affairs. When he was alive you were trumpeting Christopher Nash as the great love of your life and yet here you are only seven months later, shacked up with a boy half his age, newly pregnant to him and bleeding him dry of every cent he can lay his hands on.' His scathing voice raking her expression of surprise with contempt, he added, 'Oh, yes, I know that he's taken on two part-time jobs to buy your expensive loyalty, regardless of the fact that his studies are suffering! He's too blind to realise that your loyalty is assured by his surname. Why should you care if he gets his qualifications with honours or not at all? It's not what he could be but who he is that interests you. I bet you've calculated his net worth as a Stone down to the last dollar! But know this: if he marries you he won't get a single cent of my money!'

Claudia was speechless with guilt and dismay. Mark had been stubbornly adamant that he would not touch the trust-fund living allowance that his father had allocated for his studies—'apron strings', he had called it, and she knew that he paid her for his room and board through his job at a pizza takeaway, but she had not known about a second job. In her self-absorption she had vaguely protested when he brought her pretty fripperies—perfume and flowers and luxurious titbits to tempt her meagre appetite—but he was so cheerfully determined for her to enjoy them for their own sake that she had closed her mind to the implications of his having spare cash to spend on her.

She took a deep breath. This had gone quite far enough. 'Mr Stone,' she said huskily, 'you have it all wrong. Of course I'm not in love with your son——'

He laughed harshly. 'You're not telling me anything I don't already know. A pity I didn't come with a tape recorder; I'm sure Mark would find this very enlightening.'

'And he is not in love with me,' she continued steadily.

'He only thinks he is? Oh, yes, I know that too, Miss Lawson. That kind of infatuation makes him very easy to manipulate, doesn't it? Your years as a racing groupie obviously serve you well when it comes to insinuating yourself where you don't belong. A pity you encouraged the love of your life to spend so much on you when he was alive—he might not have left you so destitute when he died. This place must be quite a come-down from the five-star hotels you and your drunken groupie friends used to regularly smash up during race parties——'

Claudia clenched her hands at her sides to stop herself lashing out at his mocking face, her whole body trembling with a violent, repressed rage. It might not be much in *his* eyes but she had struggled hard against tremendous odds to make a home for herself here, to build a secure background for her baby in the midst of a shatteringly insecure world. He had no right to taint it with his contempt. But she would not beg for his understanding. No, he deserved to suffer a little of the torment he had offered her!

'Do you always believe what you read in the papers, Mr Stone?' she attacked. 'I wouldn't have thought you so gullible——'

'It's my son who's the gullible one. He always was too soft for his own good.'

The casual disrespect for Mark was another reason to hate him. 'For his own good—or for yours? You know, Mr Stone, the ironic thing is that I didn't really believe him when he told me about you. I thought he was exaggerating. I even suggested that he get in touch with you to try to work things out.'

The blue eyes looked stunningly unimpressed by the information. 'You suggested a reconciliation? How touching! And how profitable for you if Mark could be welcomed back into the family bosom...and bank-balance.'

It was like hitting her head against a brick wall. No—a Stone wall, decided Claudia hysterically. Who could have believed that a simple misunderstanding could mushroom into a confrontation of such nightmare proportions? The labyrinthine conversation had taken so many twists and turns away from the clearly illuminated path of the truth that she felt dizzy and disorientated. He confused and enraged her, standing there so perfectly groomed, so perfectly righteous so...so *perfect* while she floundered in the hopeless knowledge that nothing she could say would convince him that she was anything but a mercenary, opportunist tramp.

'But perhaps there is another alternative,' he murmured into the sizzling silence. 'One that might be just as profitable for you...'

'If you're going to offer to pay me off you can forget it!' said Claudia fiercely, the headache that had dragged her out of bed that morning returning with a vengeance. 'I want you out of my house. *Now*!'

'*Your* house?' The mirthless smile reappeared. 'I understand that it belongs more to a finance company than to you and the repayments must take a large chunk of your benefit money. You *are* on a welfare benefit these days, aren't you, Miss Lawson? You certainly seem to have made no attempt to find a job in the last few months. I suppose you decided that getting pregnant was a good way to avoid having to earn a living in the foreseeable future now that the government is tightening up on persistent free-loaders on the welfare state. I wonder how the welfare people would view your cohabiting with a man who is obviously supporting you with money and gifts?'

'I am not a cheat!' Claudia flared, lifting her pointed chin, the flecks in her eyes blazing angrily. It was shaming enough that because of her difficult pregnancy she had been forbidden to work and had to accept what she saw as charity to live. To have him rub her nose in it was doubly humiliating. 'The social welfare department knows all about Mark! So don't think you can blackmail me if your bribes fail.'

'If?' He was swift to pick up her slip of the tongue. 'So you *are* willing to consider a bid—if it's high enough?' He named a figure that took her breath away. Unfortunately it also exploded the last shreds of her self-control.

Later, the sequence of events played themselves over and over in her agonised head—her attacking him with all the vile words that had used to make her blush when she heard Chris use them at the track whenever he lost a race through someone else's incompetence. Her shoving at his immovable bulk, raining blows on his impervious chest, his catching her elbow to try and calm her hysteria, her wrenching away, slipping, falling jarringly on her side...

She lay, dazed, on the threadbare carpet as he dropped to his knees beside her, that pale, implacably stony face exhibiting the first jagged cracks of emotion, the blue eyes icing with shock as his hand hovered above her hip.

'Are you all right?'

'Don't touch me!' If he touched her she would shatter. The fear that had haunted her since Chris's violent death solidified into an agonised certainty that she had been too terrified to entertain before this moment. Since the incessant vomiting of her first month of her pregnancy she had been waiting, dreading, hoping and praying that this moment would never come. The moment when she would have to pay for the sins of her past. But not this way, please, God, not this way... She moaned.

'Miss Lawson—Claudia, are you hurt?' She heard the reluctant horror in his voice, the grudging concern.

'Go away, leave me alone...' A ripple of pain shuddered through her body, breaking her words up into fragmented syllables as she closed her eyes and turned her head away from him, away from the cruelty of the world.

'I can't do that. Not when you might be hurt. Is it here? Is it your baby?' His hand lightly feathering against her swollen belly made her convulse with a pain that was more mental than physical. She sobbed and heard him curse under his breath and shift, felt the skirt of her dress delicately lifted. Her eyes flew open, a little mew of humilitated protest dying on her dry lips as he carefully tucked the fabric back over her curled legs and leaned closer to stroke the damp strands of hair back from her sweaty brow as he murmured reassuringly,

'There's no blood, Claudia. You're not bleeding and your waters haven't broken. Don't cry—you're not alone. I'll take care of you. Who's your doctor?'

Oh, God, he was as implacable in his gentleness as he was in his rage, even though he despised her. Claudia's head swam and her bones ached and at that moment she gave up hope.

'I'm going to be sick——' she gritted through clenched teeth.

She was, miserably, and afterwards he lifted her very gently on to the firm couch, sitting beside her, stroking her shuddering body soothingly as he made an emergency call on the cellphone that he had produced from his inside pocket.

When the call was finished he bathed her face with a cool, damp cloth and talked softly to her, not seeming to care that she wasn't listening, her blank eyes shuttered, her whole being focused inside herself, preparing for the pain that she knew was to come.

He rode in the ambulance, too, and for some inexplicable reason she instinctively clung to his hand, only letting him break away when the hospital emergency staff finally persuaded him that his insistent presence in the examining-room was interfering with her treatment. The rest of that day and part of the night degenerated into a blur of pain and horror so that when next she woke she thought it had all been some unlikely nightmare.

Then she registered the cool white room, and explored the exhausted emptiness inside her and knew it had all been real. Too real. She closed her stinging eyes and when she opened them again the doctor was there. Not the young emergency doctor but the consultant gynaecologist from the hospital's pregnancy clinic whose special patient she had been.

She received his kindly expression of sympathy apathetically, remaining dry-eyed at the information that her baby had been a son. Only when he sat on the chair beside the bed and began to question her about her activities in the last few days did she show a flicker of emotion.

'Had you noticed the baby moving much, Claudia, recently?'

She looked down at her fingers, picking at the bleached white sheet folded across her breasts. 'Was he perfect? I mean—he wasn't...?'

'Deformed? No, Claudia. But there was no heartbeat when they brought you in—that's why the Ceasarean was necessary—speed was of the essence.' He paused, and then continued, more gently, 'I don't think you'd felt him moving for quite a while, had you, Claudia?'

The tears that had been stinging in her eyes were hot on her cheeks. 'He—he was never a very active baby during the day...it was at night that he used to kick——'

'And the last few nights?'

She blanked out the unease that she had dismissed as a pregnant woman's fancy. 'I—I've been very tired, sleeping heavily recently—I don't know. I—when I fell it must have——'

He took her restless hand from the mangled sheet. 'It wasn't the fall, my dear. I think that perhaps in your heart you know that. It wasn't anything that was any fault of yours. All the fall did was to start your premature labour. But all the indications are that your baby had been dead for several days——'

'No!' She wrenched her hand away, placing it over her flattened stomach as she denied the secret terror that had stalked her dreams. 'No—I would have known something was wrong—I would have done something——'

'I doubt that there was anything anyone could have done, Claudia. Sometimes these things happen——'

'What things? You said the baby was perfect—so it must have been me! What did I do wrong?' she cried in tearful anguish.

'You did nothing wrong, my dear,' he reassured her patiently. 'And I agree that the baby appeared physically perfect but we don't know about the rest. I did warn you at the beginning that there were some disturbing aspects to the pregnancy that could indicate that you might not carry to full term...'

'But I did everything you said,' whispered Claudia wretchedly.

'I know you did. You did everything you could for your baby, Claudia, I know that. But sometimes it's just not enough. Perhaps later, when I know more, I'll be able to give you precise reasons.' Claudia quickly pushed away the awful implications of those words. 'Meanwhile you should get as much rest as possible. Losing a baby in the later stages of pregnancy is much more traumatic than earlier miscarriage. And I know you probably don't want to hear this right now, but you need to know that the emergency doctor said that there was no indication of any chronic physical complications that would jeopardise future pregnancies. There is every chance that next time you will deliver a normal, live, healthy baby... and you won't necessarily have to have it by Caesarean...'

'*Next* time...?' Claudia couldn't imagine ever risking this kind of heartbreaking agony again.

'It was a mistake, you know!' she remembered achingly. 'I didn't mean to get pregnant—it was such a shock—I—do you think——?'

'No, I don't, and nor should you,' the doctor said sternly. 'Whatever your feelings at the beginning, you fought long and hard to have this baby, Claudia, and now you'll have to fight to accept this and go on. Now, shall I tell your friend he can come in and see you for a few minutes? The nurses tell me he's been out there all night pestering them, wearing a groove in the waiting-room...'

'Friend?' With Mark away she couldn't imagine who would have come to see her. Only Mark and her parents in Australia were listed as contacts on the information sheet she had filled in when she had first attended the hospital clinic.

'The very appropriately named Mr Stone. Sister Dawson says that he's as stubborn as a rock. He's not satisfied with the brief bulletins she's given him and is demanding to talk to your doctor. The emergency man has been flat out all night, and I've had a few other calls to make, but if you like I could explain to him now what's been going on——'

'No!' Claudia's voice was shrill with panic. Suddenly she had a source for all her pain. A perfect repository for all her rage and guilt. *Perfect*. How she hated that word. Hated him for being there when her body had rejected her own baby. 'No. I don't want you to tell him anything! He's not a friend—I hardly know him. I don't want him to know anything about me!'

The consultant eyed her cautiously. 'He already knows that we operated and the baby was born dead. In view of the fact that he was with you when it happened, don't you think——?'

'No, I don't.' Her agitation increased to borderline hysteria. 'Promise me you won't tell him! You have to have my permission to discuss my medical details with him, don't you? I don't give it. I don't want him here. Tell him to go away!'

He had no option but to agree, and, after a few more minutes inspecting her stitches and assessing her condition, he left. Claudia lay painfully on her side, her body curled up around her achingly empty womb. Tears seeped slowly from her under her tightly closed lids. After the gradual blossoming of joy inside her over the past few months it was a cruel shock to have her happiness snatched away as the illusion it was.

'Claudia?'

She opened her eyes to find Morgan Stone bending over her.

Even in her slightly drug-confused state she was shocked by the change in him—his rumpled haggardness, his hair uncombed, eyes red-rimmed with fatigue and the elegant suit decidedly rumpled. Then she was viciously pleased at the evidence of his long, desperate wait. He *should* be feeling desperate. *He* should be the one lying stiff and cold somewhere in the depths of the hospital, not her darling, innocent baby son...

'What are you doing here?' she demanded, smearing away her tears with an angry hand. She might have known he would arrogantly ignore the doctor's message that she didn't want to see him, she thought bitterly. The only wishes Morgan Stone cared about were his own.

'I had to see you. To see how you were. To see if you needed anything—if I can get you anything...' His mouth was a thin, crooked white line of tension.

'Yes, there's something I need—my baby back, alive and well,' she spat at him with searing contempt, trapped into the confrontation by the pain that pinned her to the bed. 'Can you do *that* for me, Mr Stone, or are you going to admit that there are *some* things your precious money will never be able to buy—like love?'

The sickly, greyish cast to his rigid, mask-like face bloomed with a dark colour across the hard, high cheek-bones; like a livid badge of shame, she thought cruelly, and yet he wore it with a kind of shattered dignity, his eyes steadily unwavering as they met the silent accusation of hers, the compassion in them causing her to recoil in a jumble of confused emotions. In her precariously vulnerable state his compassion would be even harder to bear than his contempt.

'No, I can't do that.'

'Then why are you here? My baby is dead and I feel as if I've been ripped apart with blunt knives. Is *that* what you're waiting to hear? Is that punishment enough for my daring to even exist on the same planet as your darling son, let alone share a relationship with him?'

The previously smooth, dark shadow of his jaw was now roughly uneven but beneath the overnight growth of salt-and-pepper stubble Claudia could see the clenching ripple of muscle as he absorbed the full force of her acid hatred. His tired eyes were navy with a deep-seated torment she refused to recognise as he said raggedly, 'God, no—Claudia, it was an accident. You can't believe I meant anything like this to happen——'

'Can't I?' she taunted him bitterly. 'Doesn't this very neatly resolve one of your problems? One less skeleton to sweep into the family closet. One less parasite to detach from the Stone fortune? Of course, whether Mark will thank you for murdering your own grandson to try and stop him marrying me is another question entirely!'

The blue eyes went opaque with shock and she felt a tiny sliver of guilt. But it was only what he deserved, she told herself with grief-distorted logic. Morgan Stone had taunted her with her fickleness, when in reality she had been completely faithful to Chris, even at those times she had not been so certain of his equal faithfulness to her. In fact, if he hadn't been killed they would have been married by now, in the typically flamboyant ceremony that Chris had been planning at the time of his death. Now Chris was beyond pain, denied forever the fatherhood that had been barely anticipated in his last few weeks of life.

'Is that what you're going to tell Mark?' Morgan Stone asked in a voice that sounded as hollow and echoingly empty as she felt.

'It's the truth, isn't it?' she said icily. 'You pushed me—I fell—I lost the baby. *You killed my baby*!' Her need to blame someone, anyone but herself, was desperate—essential for her survival.

'Claudia, please——'

'Oh, don't worry,' she sobbed wildly. 'You don't have to beg. I won't tell him. And if you have any feeling left for your son you won't either. You think I want to hurt him like that? You think I want him to carry around that crushing burden of guilt for the rest of his life—knowing what you did because of his friendship with me?'

She didn't want Mark hurt. The only person who should suffer, who *must* suffer, was the man whose arrogant contempt had destroyed her baby.

'Claudia—I——' He stopped, and made an inarticulate sound, gesturing helplessly with his lean hands. For all his fierce self-restraint he looked...lost. And suddenly she felt a terrifying surge of unwelcome empathy—the sharing of that most basic parental fear of loss of a child—whether baby or a grown adult. No, oh, no, she couldn't let herself share anything with him, feel anything for him...she had to make him go away—*now*...before she weakened any further...

'Just get out. I feel violated by your just being in the same room as me,' she told him in a listlessly pale voice suddenly drained of all life. 'And you don't have to worry about Mark and me. We're not going to get married. There was never any question of it anyway—I would have told you that in the first place if you hadn't bullied your way in like a cheap thug and started flinging insults around. I would have told you, too, that he's gone away for a week with friends—won't be back until next Sunday...'

Morgan Stone shifted sharply and, in case it was with triumphant relief, she gave the knife one last, deliberate twist. 'So I guess that for the want of some patience your grandson was lost. Maybe one day I'll be glad that I didn't bring another child of your blood into the world. Right now, the way I'm feeling, I really don't care if I never see you or your son ever again.'

CHAPTER TWO

CLAUDIA looked into the bleary eyes of a famous female rock star and endeavoured to make her lie as sincere as humanly possible.

'I'm sure nothing is going on. The maid must have misinterpreted a perfectly innocent gesture from your husband. She was upset, she knew she was somewhere she wasn't supposed to be—so she blurted out the first thing that came to mind to divert attention——'

'Well, it was a bloody lousy thing to say. Silly bitches like that shouldn't be allowed to work in hotels. If you won't fire her I'll talk to the general manager. He sure as hell won't ignore me——'

'Naturally the girl will be removed from her duties,' Claudia lied smoothly, endeavouring not to wince at the raw language. It was mild compared to the rock star's initial outburst, compounded of tears, rage and, Claudia suspected, a dangerous mixture of alcohol and exhaustion. Eliza Mitchell was on the last leg of a world tour which had begun in her native England and the pressures were obviously catching up with her. On one level Claudia sympathised with the famous guest's outraged feelings of betrayal but privately considered that they were being vented on the wrong person, and she had no intention of allowing what was evidently an ongoing marital war to jeopardise the job of an innocent and hardworking member of the hotel staff.

It took a further twenty minutes to smooth things over, and by the time she let herself out of the suite into the fifteenth-floor corridor Claudia was beginning to feel a little frazzled herself. The hotel security guard outside the door grinned at her reappearance. He had had a ringside seat when the ruckus started and had called down to the security office while defending the unfortunate maid from a hail of hotel furnishings.

'Oiled the troubled waters, Miss Lawson?'

Claudia sighed. 'Would you mind calling down for Housekeeping to send someone *experienced*—and preferably middle-aged—up to replace the vase and chairs in the penthouse suite? But wait until Miss Mitchell and her husband have gone out; she's due at a Press conference in forty-five minutes.'

'Will do, Miss Lawson. You know, you should have been a diplomat!'

'I don't have any languages,' she said, and then smiled wryly. 'Although I think Eliza Mitchell just taught me a word or two I didn't know before.'

She nodded to the two extra security men flanking the glass lift and exhaled in relief as she began the smooth descent to the ground floor. She didn't enjoy lying even when, as now, it had been made clear to her that a lie was the correct and required response to Eliza Mitchell's hysteria. The woman knew the truth but was unwilling to admit it to herself or anyone else. So Claudia had obligingly provided her with the opportunity to avoid facing it. As public relations co-ordinator for the Baron HarbourPoint she often had to soothe over awkward situations with a view to the hotel's reputation but today's lie had probably been the biggest and most distasteful she had ever been called on to produce.

Her eyes darkened and she turned to look out over the panorama of Wellington harbour revealed by the glass wall of the lift, blankly unseeing of the armada of small boats welcoming several naval frigates sailing into Wellington for navy anniversary celebrations.

No, not the biggest lie. The biggest lie she had ever told had been the ugly one she had flung at Morgan Stone in that spare hospital room two years ago. A lie soon regretted but never redeemed. She had preferred to push it away. Pretend that it—and he—had never existed. But even the pretence was a lie. In a dark, unacknowledged corner of her mind she knew that she had committed a crime against an innocent man and, just as she had condemned him to carrying the death of a child on his conscience, so she had condemned herself to the perpetual burden of remembrance.

The lift doors opened and Claudia's heels clicked against the polished marble floor as she crossed the wide foyer towards the curving reception desk.

'Claudia? *Claudia*?'

A firm male hand on her arm halted her progress. Claudia turned, staring blankly at the man who had accosted her until he grinned familiarly.

'I know it's been a long time, Claudia, but not *that* long, surely? It's me—Mark Stone, remember? We used to live together.' And as she still failed to react to the joke his handsome face sobered. 'Hey, I didn't mean to rake up bad memories or anything, but it's just so great to see you again...'

Claudia was so appalled by the apparition that she had conjured up by her brooding that it took her a further few seconds to adjust to the fact that she was facing solid reality, not a fantasy from her own guilty conscience.

'Hello, Mark,' she said huskily, forcing a smile as she looked up into his incredibly handsome face. It was almost two years to the day, she realised with a pang, since she had seen him. 'I'm sorry, my mind was elsewhere. I—— What are you doing here?' Her heart was suddenly fluttering with panic as her eyes slid nervously around the foyer.

'Business appointment—I'm meeting someone who's staying here. What are you...?' He looked down at her clothes and did a discreet double-take at the name badge she wore. 'You *work* here—at the hotel?'

Her smile came naturally this time, the fluttering in her chest subsiding a little. *He was alone.* 'I'm in charge of public relations for the hotel.'

'That's fantastic! And you live in Wellington now. Why haven't you looked me up? I told you to, if you were ever in town...'

'I've only been here a couple of months; I'm still getting my bearings,' Claudia prevaricated. She could hardly tell him that she had tried to refuse her transfer from the Baron LakePoint in Auckland to avoid just this eventuality. However, her request for another posting had been denied and she had told herself that she was being unnecessarily cautious. New Zealand's capital city was a big place and it was hardly likely that she would run into Morgan Stone or his son.

'You never replied to any of my letters either,' Mark continued. 'I worried about you, you know—whether you were mad at me for leaving so suddenly and so soon after your—you lost the baby...'

'Of course not; I understand,' she murmured, her heart sinking at the hint of hurt in his expression. The last thing she needed was to shoulder another burden of guilt!

Unfortunately, she had understood all too well why Morgan Stone had suddenly decided to mend fences with his son, offering the imminent prospect of a business partnership if Mark would move back to Wellington. Mark's swift departure, three weeks after she had lost the baby, had followed his sheepish explanation that he had visited his maternal grandparents during his holiday and they had persuaded him that his father might be willing to compromise after all.

'Things were pretty hectic for me after you left—taking that hotel course, deciding to sell the house—and I'm afraid that letter-writing got pushed on to the back-burner,' she said, trying not to let her eyes waver from the innocent enquiry of his. She had been taken aback by his uncomplicated pleasure on seeing her but now she could afford to relax a little. *He knows nothing*, she realised with relief. She had never told him about his father's visit that day or the circumstances of her miscarriage, and now it seemed that Morgan Stone had been equally silent on the subject.

'Well, you're looking great now, I must say. Terrific, in fact!' Mark still had all of his youthful enthusiasm and in spite of herself Claudia was warmed by his outrageous flattery, although she could hardly have looked worse than she had during the time that he knew her! She knew that she looked a different woman from that pale, sickly creature. The cream and navy hotel uniform for female front-of-house staff suited her dark colouring and slim-hipped, long-legged figure and thanks to the hotel gym and the excellent meals provided for live-in staff she was stronger and healthier than she had ever been in her life.

'You're looking pretty good yourself,' she said, noting the beautifully cut suit that enhanced his Greek-god looks and the sleek grooming that had superseded the casual sloppiness of his student days. 'Quite the sophisticated man-about-town.'

He grinned at her teasing. 'You must be mixing me up with my father—he's the sophisticate; I'm just a pup in comparison.'

The easy reference set Claudia's nerves on edge, as did the thread of pride interwoven through Mark's humorous words. Was this the same young man who'd used to rail against his father's rigid intransigence and despise him for his manipulative coldness?

'Hey, how about we meet later and have a chat about old times?'

Old times? Claudia flinched inwardly. She looked at her watch, and automatically dropped into her professional persona. 'Er—well, I'm really pretty busy, Mark. I have a few meetings myself and then I'm con-

ducting a back-of-house tour for some of our guests and
then I have to attend a champagne-tasting we've arranged for a few of our regulars . . .'

To her surprise and relief, Mark accepted her brush-
off without argument, a little spark of mischief glowing
in his hazel eyes as he shrugged.

'OK. Some other time, perhaps. Lovely to see you
again, Claudia. Cheerio!'

Slightly stunned at the ease with which she had evaded
what could have turned into an awkward and painful
encounter, Claudia watched him go. She couldn't believe it was that easy.

It wasn't.

Six hours later Claudia was laughing over a glass of
Charles Heidsieck with a tall blond man of greyhound
elegance when she felt a presence at her elbow. She
turned, the remnants of laughter glimmering in her
brown eyes.

'Told you I'd see you again, Claudia.' Mark was full
of glee at his surprise.

'If you're boasting about gatecrashing, Mark, I should
warn you that this is Simon Moore, our general
manager,' Claudia said wryly as she introduced the two
men, briefly mentioning Mark's status as a student
boarder in her home.

Mark lifted his hands. 'I'm strictly legit. Your invitation to guests said they were welcome to bring a couple
of guests. I'm one of Tony's.' He pointed out his stocky,
middle-aged companion, already talking with keen
interest to one of the unattached women attending the
tasting, as the man he had earlier met for lunch.

'Don't worry, he's also legit,' he added wickedly when
he saw Claudia's glance flick to the other man's left hand,
wrapped around the stem of his glass. 'He's divorced
and up for grabs. If you like, I'll introduce you, Claudia.'

'You may as well forget the matchmaking,' Simon
commented with his easy smile. 'Claudia's as married to

the hotel business as I am, for which I'm grateful. She's certainly a dedicated employee—she's always brimming with ideas and she's done wonders for the HarbourPoint's image in the short time she's been here.'

'Why, thank you, Simon,' Claudia murmured sweetly, thinking he was laying it on a bit thick.

His brown eyes twinkled. 'Just indulging in some good PR, my dear. As you so frequently point out, blowing one's own trumpet produces a single, often discordant note, but blowing each other's creates a harmonious orchestra. Well, I suppose I'd better keep circulating.' He patted Claudia on the shoulder as he nodded to Mark. 'It was interesting to meet you, Mr Stone. I hope you enjoy your visit to the hotel.'

'I'm sure I shall,' Mark murmured as the other man moved away. 'Is there something going on there, Claudia?'

'He's my boss, Mark.' Claudia was startled by his suggestion. She and Simon got on extremely well but there had never been a hint of anything more personal between them.

'So? He's single, isn't he? And good-looking, and a smooth talker. Or are you already involved with someone else?'

'No, I'm not, nor do I want to be——'

'Mmm, maybe he is just a little bit *too* smooth,' he commented consideringly, eyeing Simon's effortless integration into the small crowd. 'It would be hard to know whether he's sincere or not. Maybe you're right to ignore any interest from that quarter.'

'Mark!' Claudia protested laughingly. 'There isn't any interest, from either side.' From the way he had slipped back into his teasing protectiveness it was as if the intervening years had never existed. But they had. And they precluded any closer friendship now. 'And if there were it would be none of your business,' she pointed out mildly.

'Just taking a friendly interest, Claudia,' he grinned. 'So...' he cosied up a little closer and tapped her glass with his '...here's to renewing old friendships. Now tell me, what have you been up to for the last two years, while I've been becoming a mini-tycoon? I guess that hotel course paid off in spades for you, huh?'

She glanced around, thinking to tell him that she was here on duty rather than for private amusement and ought to circulate herself when her gaze collided with a frigid blue one across the room. There, talking to the man she could remember only as Tony, was Morgan Stone, and as she looked at him he broke off his conversation and began to move. Towards her.

The world and everything in it vanished, except for that approaching blue void. She was tumbling; weightless, helpless as it rushed towards her, swallowing her will to speak, to think, to move. She was cold, so cold that her hands and feet felt like lumps of ice.

She heard Mark say something, and tried to turn to him but she couldn't, trapped by that approaching nightmare. She had imagined this moment often, but always it was with herself in control, prepared, braced to do what she knew had to be done. Not like this. Without warning. She felt a strange cold tingling creeping up the back of her skull and knew it was a symptom of shock. For one cowardly moment she wondered if she was going to be able to escape humiliation by fainting, but her natural resilience was too strong. Colour flared violently back into her white face as Morgan Stone halted in front of them.

'Well, Mark, I'm here. And this, I presume, is my surprise.' His voice was as deep, as crisp and darkly sardonic as she remembered.

Surprise didn't even begin to cover it. As Claudia's mind began to function again she could interpret the tightness of his jaw, the pin-point narrowness of his pupils stranded in the ice-pack of his eyes. His shock was as great as hers; he was just a little better at handling it.

'Yeah. This is the lady I lived with for a while when I was in Auckland.' Mark put his arm across her shoulders. 'She was a real darling. I couldn't have wished for a more accommodating landlady.'

Claudia wished he could have worded it differently. His innocent words were more bricks in the wall of misunderstanding.

'An accommodating landlady is an experience that every student should be granted on his road to maturity,' his father agreed blandly.

Oh, God, what did that mean? Claudia's icy hands began to sweat. She loved her job. She didn't want to lose it over an ugly public scene. She licked her dry lips, and then found Morgan Stone staring at her mouth. His eyes slid further, to her neat breasts, cloistered behind the navy jacket and the flat stomach revealed by her tailored skirt. Was he remembering her body as it had been, over-ripe to bursting with her child? Claudia couldn't help a tiny defensive movement of her hands and his eyes rose to her face again. This time there was something smouldering there that made her afraid. Was he going to challenge her? Was her lie at last going to catch up with her?

'Well, Mark? Aren't you going to introduce me to the lady?'

Was there just the tiniest hesitation before *lady*? Claudia didn't care. She only knew that she had received a temporary reprieve. He was willing to pretend they'd never met.

'Dad, I'd like you to meet the lovely Claudia Lawson. She's the public relations co-ordinator here at the hotel. Claudia, this is my father, Morgan Stone.'

Her worst nightmare held out his hand and Claudia had no choice but to take it politely. His palm was hot in contrast to her cold, damp one, and she saw his eyes flicker at the realisation. She half expected him to smirk at the betraying evidence of her nervousness but instead he did something that shocked her to her toes.

He lifted her limp hand to his mouth, pressing his lips against the blue veins tracing beneath the skin from the back of her wrist to her knuckles, his thumb moving gently, almost reassuringly, against her palm. Claudia's eyes widened on his bent head and when he rose to his full height again she felt her flush deepen, struggling against the impulse to snatch her hand out of his and wipe it against her skirt. He had to be mocking her, he *had* to be!

'Cut it out, Dad,' Mark chuckled, seeming to see nothing odd in his arrogant ogre of a father performing a gracious, old-fashioned salute to a strange woman. 'You're making her blush. And you're wasting your time trying to impress her because she's already spoken for.'

'Oh?' Morgan Stone still held her hand and his fingers tightened, his eyes moving sharply between his son and his flustered captive. He was just as big and hard and masculine as she remembered but now she saw that there was a distinct frosting of grey in the short, midnight-dark hair, a few more lines radiating out from his un-forgettably brilliant eyes.

'He means the general manager just told him I was wedded to my job,' Claudia said quickly.

'I see. Then you're not married?'

Was that a dig at her past? 'Not yet,' she said, extremely wary of his pleasantness.

'Oh. Does that mean that you're engaged?'

She wished she had a convenient fiancé to stop this polite interrogation in its tracks.

'No,' she admitted stiffly.

'I see.'

What did he see? Claudia pointedly flexed her fingers and he relinquished his warm clasp. At least she wasn't cold any more. She was distressingly hot—and thoroughly confused by his blandness.

'Did you move to Wellington recently, Claudia?'

His use of her first name was disconcerting, as was his innocent expression of enquiry. That hauntingly contemptuous 'Miss Lawson' still lingered in her memory. 'I was transferred from the Baron LakePoint in Auckland two months ago,' she said tautly.

'By your request?'

The implication was unmistakable. 'No—I was quite happy at the LakePoint,' she said firmly. 'It just happens to be part of management policy to regularly rotate staff to other hotels within the group.'

'An offer you couldn't refuse?' he murmured reflectively. 'Is this your first visit to Wellington?'

What was he getting at? Did he think she might have been regularly sneaking into town to see Mark behind his back? Her answer was clipped with angry frustration. 'Yes.'

'I see. And where are you living at the moment?'

'Here, at the hotel, but it's only a temporary measure while I settle into the job. I'm looking for a suitable place of my own to rent...' Her cool façade slipped as she realised how much she was revealing and she demanded with equal bluntness, 'Where *you* live?' She would make a note to steer well clear of the location.

'I have a home over on Marine Drive.'

So he lived in one of the hillside residences on the opposite shore of Port Nicholson. Claudia was surprised. She would have thought that the kind of workaholic Mark had painted him as would prefer to live in the city centre, at Oriental Bay or one of the other exclusive, convenient, inner-city suburbs. There was the view, of course, and the eastern bays were within comfortable commuting distance of the city by car or ferry, but for a man who apparently spent little time at home and had no hobbies but his work she thought the view and the beaches were probably wasted on him.

'And are *you* married?' She followed up his calm reply with another goading question.

His dark eyebrows ascended sharply and Mark made a muffled choking sound that could have been laughter. The answer, when it came, was a deliberate parody of her earlier one.

'Not yet.'

'Oh, does that mean you have someone in mind?' she cooed, equally mocking. 'Who's the un—er—lucky...lady?'

He looked at her consideringly for a long moment, until she began to regret her stupidity in challenging him. Then suddenly he smiled, making him look all the more dangerous.

'I regret to say that underneath this urbane exterior beats the crude heart of a commoner,' he said, laying a hand across the breast of his dark suit. 'If and when I marry again it'll be to a woman rather than a lady. Ladies are for pedestals; women are for wives. It's a fine line but a definite one...rather like the difference between men and boys.'

'I didn't know there was one,' said Claudia crushingly, looking down her haughty nose at him, a difficult deed to accomplish since he was at least six inches taller than her, even though she was wearing her party heels.

'Really?' he drawled, completely uncrushed. 'My dear Claudia, you *have* been running with the wrong crowd.'

So intent had she been on the silent interchange which shadowed the verbal jousting that she had quite forgotten Mark, until he shifted uneasily beside her.

'Hey, you're not arguing, are you? I thought you two would get on like a house on fire. After all, you both have something in common—me!'

His feeble joke produced a tiny, telling silence, and Claudia was about to rush into the breach with something foolish when Morgan Stone spoke again, still in that slow, easy drawl.

'Oh, there's a fire all right, Mark, isn't there, Claudia? We're just not sure whether to douse it or feed it.'

'Huh?'

'Speaking of dousing, Claudia is out of champagne and I haven't tasted any yet.' The soft comment jogged Mark into over-eager action, the sophisticated air he had been busily projecting dissolving in his puppyish desire to please.

'Oh, hey, let me get that for you...' He removed the empty glass from Claudia's nerveless fingers and slipped away. She didn't even remember having drained it and now she suddenly felt light-headed as she confronted Morgan Stone without the protection of his son's presence. What had he meant about a fire?

'You're looking very beautiful—no wonder he's so enchanted to see you again.'

'I—I beg your pardon?' Claudia was sure she must have misheard that husky ripple of sound.

He ignored her wide-eyed shock, studying the way her silky black hair shaped her head and flared out around her neck in a thick, blunt bob that just licked forward at her jawline. 'No, perhaps not beautiful. Very lovely. Another case of subtle but definite difference. You look younger with your hair short—young and carefree.'

Carefree was the last thing she felt right now and maybe her expression told him as much for he stopped looking at her in that disturbing fashion and said quietly, 'You never told him what happened. You could have used the information to widen the breach between us, but you didn't. I thank you for that.'

'I—I thought *you* might,' she stumbled, disorientated by his stunning boldness in cutting to the heart of her unease.

'You said you didn't want me to,' he said simply.

'And what I want *mattered*?' she said incredulously, adding sarcastically, 'Of course, it had nothing to do with suiting your own interests.'

His blue eyes never flinched. 'I don't deny it. If he'd talked to me about it, perhaps I would have told him. But he has never confided in me. We weren't on close or comfortable terms with each other for quite a while after he came back. There were...adjustments to be made on either side. When he talked about you it was always in general terms. He mentioned your losing a baby, but he never admitted or indicated in any way that it had been his. In fact he seemed so willing and relieved to come home that I thought what happened must have shocked him out of his infatuation. I thought it was kinder to both of you not to interfere——'

'Not interfere! What did you call pestering me in the hospital? And suddenly offering Mark a partnership when you'd refused to even discuss letting him have any sort of involvement in your business.' That was as informative as Mark had got about the argument that had caused the split.

'Being humanly fallible. Being willing to admit I was wrong. I wanted him to have choices——'

'Knowing that he'd choose not to stay with me——'

'If he'd loved you he would have stayed—or brought you with him,' he said bluntly. 'It was his decision to come back alone. And you had admitted to me that you didn't love him.'

She looked away. Why was she arguing with him? Compounding the lies that she already regretted?

'However much you resent me, Claudia,' he said quietly, 'I only did what I thought was best at the time for my son. And, looking at you now, I think that perhaps it was also best for you...'

'I suppose you think it was best for my baby, too!' she blurted fiercely, the ache of emptiness that she thought had been filled momentarily returning to haunt her.

Some of her pain must have shown in her face because he placed his hand on her waist, turning her so that she was facing him directly, her back to the room. 'I'm sorry. I wasn't being dismissive of your loss. I, of all people, know how much you suffered. That was why I visited you. I wasn't pestering you. No one else came to see you.'

'I didn't need your pity then and I certainly don't need it now!' she denied proudly.

'No. But you did need something from me. Money. Quite an outrageous amount of it, in fact,' he pointed out pitilessly, in direct contrast to the gentle restraint of his touch on her waist. Claudia felt her defiance flee before her shame.

Morgan Stone hadn't gone away meekly when she had ordered him to. He hadn't left her alone. For three days he had continued to visit, bringing flowers and fruit and news of the outside world, even though Claudia had resolutely refused to even look at him, closing her eyes and putting on the headphones that hung above her bed.

When she had recovered sufficiently to realise that she was in a private rather than public hospital and that Morgan Stone had arranged to pay her bills she had further reason to fiercely resent his manipulation of her life. She could never have afforded the extravagance of private care for herself and the envelope that he had handed her as he left on the third day turned out to be the final, supreme humiliation. When she had listlessly opened it she had found inside a cheque for several thousand dollars and a brief note suggesting that she reconsider her relationship with his son in the light of her financial independence ... and the fact that Mark would be dependent on his father's goodwill for the foreseeable future. The fact that the cheque wasn't post-dated had merely underlined his certainty as to her greed.

Claudia hadn't had the chance to throw his conscience-money back in his arrogant face. She'd never seen him again, and, cheated of the chance to salvage her pride, the only revenge left had been to keep his money, to extract payment for his imagined sins in the only way he seemed to appreciate: cold, hard cash.

Later she had realised the reason for his abrupt departure. He had discovered that Mark was at his parents' home and had flown back to Wellington to protect his investment! Mark had been so over the moon about his father's startling and apparently unique reversal of his earlier decision that Claudia had quietly relinquished her futile fantasies of furthering her revenge against an innocent man, and sent him on his way with her best wishes for the future.

'Did you expect me to refuse your blood money in some grand gesture of defiance?' she sneered defensively. 'Well, I didn't. I spent it, every last cent!'

'So my bank-statement informed me,' he said calmly, his eyes on her flushed face. 'I hope you used it wisely.'

'Of course I did. I spent it on clothes and jewellery and having a good time,' she answered flippantly.

'Did you, Claudia?'

Why did she get the feeling that beneath his gravity he was amused? She glared at him. He couldn't possibly know that she had used the money to pay for her hotel course at the technical institute and to support herself until she'd gained the qualifications that got her her job with Baron's.

'Isn't that what you expected a cheap tramp like me to do?'

'Oh, not cheap, Claudia, never cheap,' he murmured. 'I think that whatever you thought I expected you to do you would do the exact opposite, just to punish me for my presumption.' His perception was as unnerving as his calmness. 'As you pointed out at the time, I didn't know enough about you to make any judgements on your character.'

'But you did it anyway!'

'As I said, I'm fallible,' he shrugged. 'I have a strong will and a hot temper. It can be a lethal combination. It's what caused me so much strife when Mark grew old enough to challenge my authority. I like to think that I've mellowed a little with age...'

'*Mellowed*?' Claudia struggled with a quite inappropriate desire to laugh. A few grey hairs were one thing, but she couldn't imagine a genial Morgan Stone, however venerable his years.

'You think I exaggerate?' he murmured crookedly.

'I've seen no evidence of it!' She looked him up and down in an insulting fashion, trying not to notice the way his lean, densely muscled body was flattered by the tailoring of his suit. If anything he looked physically even tougher than he had two years ago.

'That's because you're afraid to look. You're too busy hiding from the past. Why don't you come out from behind your defences, Claudia? You might be surprised at what you find——'

'Where's Mark with that champagne?' she interrupted shrilly, totally unnerved by his unwillingness to fight.

'He's very diplomatically giving us time to get acquainted,' Morgan replied, shifting to block her view of the room. 'He wants us to like each other. It seems to be important to him. Don't disappoint him, Claudia.'

It sounded almost like a warning. 'Or what?' she demanded acidly.

'Or I might feel obligated to explain the real reason for your lack of enthusiasm for meeting me...'

'You'd tell him—*now*?' Claudia was stunned by the suggestion.

He shrugged. 'Why don't we discuss it over dinner?'

She was even more stunned. '*Dinner*? With *you*?'

'And Mark...with his fiancée, of course.'

'Mark's engaged?' Her question jerked out involuntarily.

'He hasn't told you?' The cynical gleam in his narrowed eyes switched on a light in her overheated brain.

'We've hardly exchanged a few words. We only met again this morning,' she said stiffly. 'I have no intention of seeing him again if that's what this is all about. So whether he's engaged or not is irrelevant.'

'What if he wants to see you?'

'I'll tell him no!'

'And if he doesn't take no for an answer?'

'Why, is it a family trait to ride roughshod over people?' she said snidely. 'Look, Mr Stone——'

'Morgan. My name is Morgan. He's coming back towards us.' His voice lowered and this time the threat was shockingly succinct. 'If you don't want me to rake up the awkward past I suggest that you co-operate.'

'That's blackmail!' Claudia gaped at him. He must be insane. All that unbridled power over the destinies of other people had evidently rotted his reason. 'Morgan,' she purred, suddenly taking great pleasure in the familiarity, a heady sense of her own power overtaking her former wariness, 'haven't you got this completely the wrong way round? You have far more reason to fear the truth coming out than I do. *I'm* the one who could blackmail *you*!' Her triumph was ineffably smug and resulted in an indefinable tension in the man opposite.

'You could, Claudia, but would you?'

She lowered her dark lashes as if thinking, her eyes shot with gold as she studied his impassive face through their silky screen, savouring her dominance over him. Her smile curved in secret satisfaction, revealing a dimple in her left cheek, and she heard his sharp intake of breath as she lifted her head to stare boldly at him, all honey eyes and taunting, rose-pink mouth, unknowingly sensual in her very feminine arrogance. 'I might!'

'I dare you!' he said softly, and before good sense could rescue her from her unaccustomed attack of reck-lessness Morgan Stone had side-stepped her and was ac-cepting a glass of champagne from his son and toasting her with it.

'Claudia was just suggesting that we dine together this evening. What do you say, Mark? Perhaps you can call Serita and we can make a night of it!'

CHAPTER THREE

'WHY are you doing this?' Claudia demanded fiercely, trying to disguise her temper with a polite smile as she moved stiffly across the polished floor.

'Dancing with you? You said you liked to dance.' Morgan Stone turned her with a delicate but firm pressure of the strong hand splayed across her naked back. What on earth had possessed her to wear a halter-neck gown?

'I was talking about this...this *farce* of a dinner!' Claudia gritted.

'You have only yourself to blame for that, Claudia. I did give you the option of meeting on neutral territory...but you took the coward's way out and your lies were what compromised you, not me...'

Coward. Lies. The accuracy of his thrust cut deeply into her pride. Those two words summed up her whole relationship with Morgan Stone. If only she hadn't panicked earlier, when he had come out with that outrageous remark about dining together, but she had been terrified of what he might say next if she denied suggesting it. Calling the bluff of a man as tough and seasoned as Morgan Stone had been a very bad mistake. Instead she had pretended to remember that she was supposed to be working, making sure that the first night of a week of theme dinners that she had arranged in the main restaurant in conjunction with a floral festival being held in the city ran smoothly.

'Perfect—we can eat here at the hotel,' Morgan Stone had interposed smoothly into her hasty explanations. 'What better way for you to check the effectiveness of the atmosphere than to experience it yourself? And you'll be on hand if there are any problems...'

'Oh, I don't think——'

'If you like I'll square things with Simon.'

'Simon?' Claudia was visited again with the peculiar sense of disorientation that Morgan Stone seemed to engender in her brain.

'Moore. Your boss. We're business acquaintances. In fact we went to the same private school...'

'Oh, no!' Her exclamation was a totally involuntary breath of horror and the piercing blue eyes narrowed in humourless appreciation of her dilemma.

'I assure you the old-boy network is quite a legitimate business tool,' he commented silkily. 'Don't you approve?'

Not when the net was a poison spider's web and she the poor, struggling fly caught in its sticky embrace!

'No—I mean, you needn't bother Simon...' she said hurriedly. Especially since he would expose her excuse for the sham it was. The overall concept of the floral theme in the hotel this week had been Claudia's, and she was responsible for publicising and co-ordinating the various events, but the head chef, a temperamental man at best, would have something to say if he thought she was trying to horn in on his jealously defended territory.

'You're sure? I wouldn't like to get you into trouble,' he murmured innocently.

God, he was a mocking swine! He knew very well she had just been trying to wriggle out from under his thumb. Claudia summoned up a chilling smile.

'I'm sure. But I was going to say that I doubt we'll be able to get a table at this late stage.' She turned her attention deliberately to Mark, her voice unconsciously softening in deference to their former friendship as she tried to inject some sincerity into her regret. 'Our Nautilus restaurant is so popular it's usually booked out days in advance, especially on Friday nights during special events.'

She might have known that the truth would be no more effective than lies where Morgan Stone was concerned. What he wanted he got. She didn't care to know what form of threat, bribery or influence he had used but he hadn't merely got them a table, he had got the best in the house, in a corner of the glass-fronted restaurant where it jutted sharply out over the harbour, giving diners the feeling that they were on sea rather than land. Claudia hadn't even tasted the meal; she had been far too busy concentrating on walking the tightrope of conversation with Mark, conscious of Morgan watching her like a hawk, observing every word and move. She had been rather voluble in her nervousness, talking a lot about her career because it seemed a nice, neutral topic, not caring that she might sound ambitious to the exclusion of everything else.

'But it wasn't an option, was it?' Claudia remembered sourly now, trying to ignore the envious feminine looks that she was garnering on the dance-floor. She returned an envious look at a woman who was dancing with a plump, cheery little man. How uncomplicated other people's lives seemed to be compared to her hopelessly tangled skein of affairs. 'I didn't want to have dinner with you *anywhere*—let alone dance with you.'

'You would rather have danced with Mark?'

'He didn't ask me.'

'But he was going to.'

Her brooding gaze snapped from the contented couple twirling past them to the blunt, dark-shadowed jaw and from there bounced up to the compelling blue challenge. So that was why he had suddenly swept her into the crowd. Her impatience got the better of her.

'So what? For goodness' sake, what do you think can happen in the middle of a dance-floor?'

'You have to ask?' With a suddenness that took her by surprise his hand slid from her shoulder-blades to the hollow in the small of her back and he drew her hips against his, making her aware of their sinuous, rhythmically evocative movements, the slight arch of recoil Claudia made only emphasising the intimate fit of their lower limbs. The hand that had been decorously holding hers dropped to his lower chest, drawing her entwined fingers down between their shifting bodies, trapping them there as he leaned his chest back into her outraged torso.

'What do you think you're doing?' she whispered fiercely, feeling the heat flare under her creamy skin.

'Dancing.' His voice was a soft rumble against her ear, his hard jaw tucked against her skull. 'Why the outrage, Claudia? After all, what can happen in the middle of a dance-floor?' He spun her deftly, his thigh sliding in between hers and lingering for a fraction of a second, enough to unbalance her so that she stumbled slightly, giving him an excuse to secure her even more tightly against himself. If she hadn't been aware of him as a man before, she certainly was now. He felt as strong as he looked and held her easily, skilfully...

'Very amusing,' said Claudia, and on her next step deliberately planted her slender high heel square on the soft Italian leather of his shoe and ground it deeply. This time it was he who staggered and came to an abrupt halt in the middle of the dance-floor, swearing under his breath.

Claudia stood straight in the prison of his powerful arm, trying not to let him see how helpless she felt against the threat of his undoubted masculinity. 'Had enough already, Mr Stone? I thought you had more stamina.'

He looked down at her from his considerable height. 'Is that a challenge, Claudia?' he asked softly.

She instantly backed down at the hint of relish in his voice. 'No, of course not. I just don't like being—

being——' She floundered, trying to think of a word that adequately described what he was doing to her.

'Danced with?'

'Oh!' She glared at him furiously.

'Isn't that what we're doing with each other? Dancing around the main issue?' he continued, with a shrewdness that dismayed her. 'That issue being your unresolved feelings about the past. You say you have no intention of getting involved with Mark, but what if he also has unresolved feelings...?'

'It wasn't *my* fault that his fiancée couldn't come to-night.' Claudia was instantly defensive.

'If he even asked her...'

Claudia's eyes widened. 'That's ridiculous.'

'Is it? He leapt at the chance to come to dinner but what sensible man would want his current girlfriend and his ex-mistress sitting at the same table?' She wasn't even aware that they had started to move again, and that his hold on her was as secure as ever, her steps a fluid match for his.

'Current girlfriend? I thought you said they were engaged...'

'He and Serita have known each other for over a year and have been dating exclusively for the last six months. She's a bright and beautiful girl, warm and sweet and very good for Mark...'

Whereas Claudia had emphatically not been, was the implication.

'And how did Mark happen to meet this paragon of virtue?' she responded tartly. 'I suppose *you* introduced them...'

'As a matter of fact her father did; he's Michael Glenn, the MP...'

'And no doubt you went to school with him, too.' Claudia knew she was being bitchy but she couldn't help it. The knowledge that this man didn't consider her good enough for his son still rankled.

'Actually he did attend the same boarding-school, but not at the same time. Michael is a decade older than I am.'

'He must be near the parliamentary retirement age, then,' Claudia jabbed wickedly. 'You might not have the advantage of his political influence much longer.'

Instead of being offended Morgan laughed, the first time she had heard him do so. It was a warm, husky sound that resonated in her senses.

'If I admit that I'm going to be a creaking forty next month will that please your vengeful soul?' he grinned, seemingly untroubled by the prospect.

'You were only eighteen when Mark was born?' Claudia blurted out the startled realisation.

'Yes.' His smile tightened to the familiar crooked line. 'The same age that Mark would have become a father if your baby had survived. And I was as ill-prepared to assume the responsibilities of fatherhood as he was.'

'W-what did you do?' she asked, unwillingly fascinated by the notion of a Morgan Stone unprepared for anything.

'Married her, of course.' He met her shocked eyes coolly as he confirmed her stunned comprehension. 'Yes, I got my girlfriend pregnant when we were still students. Why do you think I was so determined to make sure that Mark wasn't condemned to repeat the mistakes of the past? Twenty years ago marriage was the only option in the society in which we moved. We were both just out of high school. Marina had no immediate family and mine refused to provide any support, financial or moral, unless we got married. So we did—but I refused to grovel for my parents' approval. I dropped my university plans and went to work to support us. It was not a success. We wanted different things out of life. If Marina hadn't died we would have been long divorced by now.'

Claudia looked away, stricken anew by the unavoidable conclusion that this man was not the ogre of her indefensible imaginings but a living, breathing human being who had endured suffering and emerged the stronger for it. A man of honour.

She swallowed. 'Morgan, I——'

'Mind if I cut in?'

Would she have told him the bald truth, right there in the middle of a public dance-floor? Claudia didn't know as she glided away with Mark, conscious of a surge of weak relief at the fresh reprieve.

'What were you talking about so intently? You hardly had two words to say to each other at the table...' Mark's curiosity obviously had more to do with his decision to cut in than a desire to dance, thought Claudia wryly. It was true she had consciously directed most of her conversation towards Mark this evening, keeping firmly on the subject of trivialities, but it had been a tactic born of fear. Morgan Stone's mere presence was enough to disrupt her normally polished self-confidence.

'I thought you wanted us to get on together,' Claudia protested lightly, turning her head so that she couldn't see the man who had relinquished her with a brooding reluctance still standing at the edge of the dance-floor.

'Get on, but not get it on,' Mark punned outrageously, his grin hinting at an uncomfortable resemblance to his father. 'I should warn you, Claudia, that Dad doesn't have a very good track record with women. He has this fatal flaw, you see. He's very competitive. He just cannot resist a challenge, but when he's conquered it he seems to lose interest...'

'You think he might see me as a challenge?' Claudia questioned with an inward shiver.

'Well, you do look have a certain touch-me-not air about you, even in that invitingly touchable dress,' he teased, running his hand over the slinky leaf-green fabric on her hip. 'And Dad can't bear being told what not to do...'

'Somehow I can't picture your father as a womaniser,' murmured Claudia uneasily, aware that if Morgan was watching them he was sure to misinterpret that stroke of her hip. 'For one thing he hasn't got the looks...'

Mark laughed. 'You, of all people, should know you can't judge a book by its cover. But you're right, he didn't used to be. The thing about Dad is that he's always been extremely single-minded. Whatever he wants he goes after with a vengeance. A lot of women find that aura of controlled aggression a real turn-on. I used to bring girlfriends home and they'd take one look at Dad and fall over themselves to get him to notice them.'

'And did he? Is that one of the reasons you fought?' Claudia couldn't help asking.

'Maybe—subconsciously it might have been...' Mark admitted slowly, as if he'd never considered the possibility before. 'Not that he ever did anything to encourage them. In those days I guess his aloofness was part of the big attraction, the way he kept everyone at an emotional distance—even me. Oh, he gave me attention when he could spare it and I got the best of everything, but I never really felt part of his real life outside in the real world—the business one he seemed to find so exciting and fulfilling. And because he had this hang-up about the expectation of inheritance making me soft I knew he'd never let me in without a fight. I would always be his son, his duty, his responsibility— never his equal, never someone to share that responsibility with. He was incapable of delegating, he always had to be in total control. I guess I made his life hell for him for a while, trying to get his attention but at the same time break away from that control. You didn't know him before so you just wouldn't realise how much he's changed in the past few years. I can hardly credit it myself. He's learned to play as hard as he works...he seems, I don't know . . . less aloof and restrained, more . . . more——'

'Mellow?' Claudia suggested wryly.

'Mellow. Yeah, I guess that's it. Mellow! More . . . *accessible*. That's what I meant about the women . . . he seems to pursue his social life these days with the same drive and aggression that used to be directed into work.'

'You almost sound disapproving,' said Claudia, amused by the role-reversal. 'Now you're finally working for him, don't you think he's got enough of his mind on the job?'

'Not *for* him, *with* him—my name's on the business now, too,' Mark corrected her, his hazel eyes glittering with youthful arrogance. 'I couldn't believe it when he agreed to add that "And Son" to the company logo. No, I just don't see why he expects *me* to want to settle down when *he's* having such an obviously good time playing the field.'

Uh-oh. 'Serita,' Claudia guessed.

Mark's dark head lifted as if prepared for criticism, then he shrugged sheepishly. 'She's a nice girl, but if Dad thinks I'm going to marry just to provide him with grandchildren while he's young enough to enjoy them——'

Claudia blanched and stumbled and before she could recover Mark had swept her out of the swaying crowd. 'Sorry, have you had enough of rolling us Stones around the floor? I see our desserts arrived so we may as well go back and join the old man . . .'

Claudia allowed Mark to seat her solicitously in front of a mouth-watering concoction of fresh raspberries decorated with stems and leaves of white and dark chocolate to look like a sheaf of roses across her plate. Her appetite, however, had deserted her.

Morgan poured her the last of the bottle of red wine which he had ordered with the superb main course.

'You look as if you need this more than I do,' he murmured provocatively. 'Your years must be catching up
with you. In your salad days I believe you used to dance
away the entire night...on table-tops, no less!'

'Once!' Claudia's response was swift and fierce. She
tempered her tone as she lifted her glass and took a
calming sip, willing herself not to over-react. '*One* table-
top—after Chris won the drivers' championship. I think
I was entitled to a little exuberance.' In truth it was Chris,
never one to deny a photo opportunity to the attendant
Press, who had swung her up on to the table and urged
her to pose for the cameras.

Mark looked from one to the other, hesitating. 'I
didn't realise you knew about Claudia and Nash, Dad...'

'I knew all about Claudia the first time I ever met
her,' his father returned smoothly, not taking his eyes
off her pale face. 'I didn't realise it was supposed to be
a secret.'

Claudia tensed. Was he going to explain when that
first time really was? Intense blue eyes measured her
nervous apprehension.

'It's not, it's simply that the Press gave Claudia a really
rough time after Nash died and she had to practically
go into hiding in order to live a normal life again,' said
Mark when she remained silent. Her knight in shining
armour—little did he know that while he still defended
her honour she had deliberately tarnished his.

'I presume you mean the fuss about his earnings—
embezzled by his manager, weren't they? And didn't his
family kick up a fuss about the prospect of you inherit-
ing his fortune—non-existent as it turned out to be?'

Claudia inclined her head stiffly. His source of information two years ago had obviously been newspaper files
so it was hardly surprising that he had had a distorted
view of her character.

At first, insulated by Chris's love, she had been amused
at the ridiculous stories about her that had circulated

regularly in the gossip columns. It was a joke between them that she was seen as some kind of jet-setting *femme fatale* whereas when they met she had been a rather quiet, serious-minded twenty-year-old whose country up-bringing had rendered her painfully naïve about the glamorous world her love for Chris catapulted her into. The naïveté had soon been crushed, but the intrinsic nature of her personality had not changed. In spite of the pressures, and the fact that her parents had never forgiven her for shaming them by flagrantly living in sin with her famous lover, Claudia had never succumbed to the temptation of believing her own Press.

'Did they ever manage to get anything back after they caught up with him, Claud?' Mark asked. 'I read in the papers that the case went to court in the States. You know, in the circumstances, you would have had a strong case for——'

'No!' Claudia quickly cut across his concern, her eyes willing him not to continue in the same revealing vein. When he appeared not to get the message she forced herself to say steadily, 'No, I—he was apparently no better at managing money for himself than he was for Chris...and anyway I just want to put all that behind me...'

Mark finally registered her tension and reacted with an unsubtle haste that made Claudia groan inwardly. He cast a guilty glance around as he leaned forward and put his hand over hers on the table, giving it a reassuring squeeze. 'Oh, sure...I understand...'

His voice was loaded with significance and she realised thankfully that he was assuming her former paranoia about the Press finding out that she had been expecting Chris's baby was the reason for her reluctance to talk. It was just the kind of sob-story that would make screaming headlines in the tabloids, even after all this time, but somehow the fear of a ravening horde of reporters baying for news was less immediately threatening than the man sitting across the table.

His fixed, suspicious gaze on their warmly clasped hands was a fresh reproach to her uneasy conscience. He was no fool; he must have realised that some sort of silent communication had just taken place and God knew what fresh misinterpretation he was dwelling on. She had to make sure that this was the last time that she encountered either of the Stones.

Deep in her guilty subconscious she had always believed that if she saw Morgan Stone again she would handle the meeting with quiet dignity, taking the opportunity that fate obviously intended to tell him the truth and express remorse for her actions. But one look into those breathtaking blue eyes and her courage had failed her. His effect on her was all mixed up with emotions she didn't even dare try to untangle. He just made her feel . . . angry, threatened, guilty, spiteful—all the things that she knew she shouldn't, that she had no right to feel. For some wicked reason, knowing that she could shock him, shake that arrogant self-confidence of his was necessary to her battered pride . . .

She used the excuse of picking up her glass again to extricate her hand naturally from Mark's.

'What circumstances were those?' She might have known that Morgan would not let the subject politely drop. She glared at him and drank, defying both him and the slight fuzzying of her brain from the reckless amount of alcohol that had helped get her through the nightmare evening.

'Er—well, there are a lot of palimony precedents in the US lawcourts,' said Mark awkwardly, obviously casting for a plausible red herring. 'And Nash being a US citizen, Claudia could have claimed a percentage of his earnings from the years they were together . . . if there had been any left to claim . . .'

'How long did you and Nash live together?' Morgan's bald question made her association with Chris sound casual and sordid. As if he didn't know the answer already.

Claudia pinned him with her most contemptuous look, the gold flecks in her eyes burning brightly with anger and pride. 'Four years,' she said slowly and succinctly. 'Four *wonderful* years.' And she promised herself that he would never discover otherwise.

'They must have been wonderful. Chris Nash wasn't known for his constancy. You must have had something very special to hold his interest so long.' His eyes raked the deep cleavage of her green halter-neck gown, the suggestion that it was her body she had used implicit in the insulting boldness of his stare.

'Dad!'

Mark's shocked protest wasn't noticed by either protagonist. Claudia, when she had recovered the wits that had fled at the blatant sexuality of that hot blue gaze, leaned forward defiantly, aware that she was making her gown even more revealing, but feeling a fierce pleasure in flaunting herself.

'We did. It's called love,' she said softly. 'You know what love is, don't you, Morgan? It's when two people make a commitment to respect and trust each other in a relationship...'

'A relationship?' he drawled. 'Oh, you mean your *affair*. It's a pity that neither of you loved strongly enough to make a formal commitment to your future.'

It was on the tip of her tongue to tell him they *had* decided to get married, but she doubted he would believe her. She had no proof and it would seem as if she was trying to ingratiate herself.

'Formal? Oh, you mean *marriage*?' she said with acid sweetness. 'But these days marriage is no guarantee of lifelong commitment. People get married for all sorts of reasons, some of which have more to do with respectability than love.' She half regretted her vicious use of his earlier confidence when his eyes flickered briefly to his bewildered son and dark colour appeared on his cheekbones, making her aware that, like his mouth, the right was slightly higher than the left.

But instead of lashing back at her with equal ferocity he sat back, lifting his half-empty glass in a cynically mocking salute. '*Touché*. Has anyone ever told you that you're beautiful when you're bitchy?'

To Claudia's disgust she blushed at the stinging compliment and he laughed.

'Has anyone ever told you that your vocabulary is as clichéd as your mind?' she said, trying to recoup her losses.

'No one as beautiful as you, Duchess.' He sipped his wine, watching her over the rim with those mesmerising eyes. 'If I'm a little blunt tonight it's because you take me by surprise. I apologise if I offended you. I'm just trying to reconcile the jet-setting racing driver's pampered mistress with the cool, classy, hardworking careerwoman image you're working so hard to project.'

What was he trying to do now? Claudia stared at him suspiciously.

'Dad... What's the matter with you? You're embarrassing her.' Mark was suspicious too, and, from his expression, not entirely pleased by the way his father was monopolising her attention.

'No, I'm not. Am I, Claudia?'

She met the challenge boldly. 'No. Once you've been harassed by sleazy journalists and groupies of both sexes the occasional crude, loud-mouthed businessman is a fairly insipid threat.'

'Insipid? I can see I'm going to have to work hard to change your opinion of me,' he murmured, the gleam of anticipation in his blue eyes sending a shiver down her bare spine.

'Now, Dad, remember you're supposed to be a *re-formed* workaholic.' Mark tried to draw their attention back to himself. 'I was just telling Claudia earlier how much more relaxed you've been in the last couple of years...'

'You mean since I stopped behaving like a petty tyrant,' his father said drily, obviously echoing words that had been thrown at him by his son in the heat of temper, 'and risked bankruptcy for the sake of boosting your boyish ego.'

'Risked bankruptcy!' Mark grinned. 'You know that sales have improved since I joined the business. You obviously needed a bit of fresh young blood among all your old fogies...'

The fact that they could banter about what, at the time, had been a bitter estrangement that had driven their relationship to the brink of destruction was an indication of the genuineness of their reconciliation, Claudia thought, and yet there was also an underlying tension to the teasing that hinted at potential conflict. Mark didn't see it in himself but he was as fiercely competitive in his way as his father, and as proud. It was Morgan's compromise that had paved the way for the resumption of their father-son relationship. How would Mark's masculine ego react if he discovered that that compromise was just another form of paternal manipulation, that both Morgan and the woman he had thought of as a friend had lied to and about him? She felt guilty enough already; no way did she want to add to that guilt by destroying the basis of their new accord.

'Of course the sales improvement had nothing to do with our increased public profile,' Morgan said mildly. 'It was we arch-conservatives who arranged the sponsorship that you're now reaping such rich rewards from, not to mention the vicarious thrills.'

Arch-conservative? Claudia couldn't help smiling to herself. In spite of the impeccable dinner-suit and the polished ease of his manners that reflected his private-school upbringing, to her Morgan Stone seemed anything but conservative.

'I didn't realise the second-hand car business was so exciting,' she couldn't help murmuring.

The two men looked at her, startled, and Claudia's faint smile faded as the silence stretched; she wondered what on earth she had said now.

'Second-hand cars?' Morgan's voice sounded strangely stifled.

'Yes. Is-isn't that what your company does?'

'Which one?'

'I didn't realise there was more than one,' said Claudia, confused as much by Mark's pained expression as his father's blandness. 'I just—Mark mentioned that your money came from second-hand car dealerships...' Her voice petered out as the blue eyes which had narrowed with scepticism on her flustered face suddenly switched thoughtfully towards his son.

Mark cleared his throat but didn't say anything.

'Is that all he told you?'

'Well—yes. We didn't talk much about his background, or you, and what there was wasn't very flattering,' she added stiffly, annoyed at being put on the defensive.

For some reason that set a smouldering spark of amusement in the coolly speculative gaze. 'No, I don't imagine you spent much of your time together *talking*...' Before she could take issue with that blatantly suggestive comment he continued, 'Yes, I own a string of franchised dealerships, but our flagship is the importation of Lamborghinis and Ferraris, Jaguars and Porsches—all kinds of classic exotic cars, both new and used. We also sponsor racing cars.'

'Racing cars?' Claudia closed her eyes briefly as she felt an echo of the rumbling vibration of the earth under the assault of thousands of horsepower, tasted the sharp, heady aroma of kerosene in the back of her tightening throat, the acrid stench of burnt rubber. The excitement had, in the end, repelled her more than it had fascinated her. Even before Chris had been killed it had taken all her courage to go to the race track, let alone smile for the cameras as he had strapped himself into one of the potentially lethal machines that he had lived to race—and ultimately loved more than life itself. She opened her eyes as Mark hastened to reassure her.

'Not Formula Ones, Claud, not what Chris used to race. Sports cars and Group One production cars. But I never mentioned it to you because I knew how upset it made you to talk about anything or anyone connected with any kind of motor racing. You felt trapped even being *in* a car for a good while afterwards. I'm sorry—Dad shouldn't have sprung it on you like that.' He gave his father a reproachful look.

Claudia smiled tensely. 'No, it's all right—honestly,' she added more convincingly as she saw his frown hover. She refused to include Morgan in her field of vision, sure he must be gloating at the sediment of her life that he was shrewdly stirring up. 'I got over that ages ago.' She pulled a face as she admitted, 'I had to. In the hotel PR trade you learn to use what connections you have and I have quite a few friends in the racing world who can add cachet to special events——'

'Rather like the old-boy network,' murmured Morgan drily, and, when she looked reluctantly at him, said quietly, 'If I caused you pain just now it was not intentional. Forgive me.'

God. Just when she was enjoying hating him he hit her with something like that. Forgive *him*? Surely it should be the other way around.

'There's nothing to forgive,' she said truthfully and made a valiant effort to prove it by acting like the consummate professional she was supposed to be, maintaining the fiction of her work by having a few words with their waiter and the *maître d'*, smoothly winding down the conversation until she could gratefully withdraw.

Her attempt to set the evening on a less personal footing by signing on her expenses for the bill when it arrived was thwarted by Morgan's stubborn insistence that she was *his* personal guest. She was frustrated and he amused when Mark circumvented the argument by picking up the pressed-flower folder containing the bill and walking off to the cashier to pay for it himself.

'While he's exercising his ego, perhaps I can walk you to your room?' suggested Morgan, standing politely behind her chair as she rose, flushed with irritation at the world in general.

'I wouldn't dream of taking you out of your way,' she said frostily, seeing it as just another tactic to keep her away from Mark.

'Oh, but you're not. I'm heading upstairs myself. Come on, you can say your farewell to Mark at the desk.' His hand on her narrow waist was as implacably firm as his words as he ushered her out of the restaurant. Claudia simmered as she walked, conscious of his towering strength at her back, forced to behave like a gracious lady when she wanted to kick and scream like a vulgar shrew.

'If you think I'm going invite you into my room for coffee you can forget it,' she snapped through a rigid smile as she responded to the friendly nod of a cabinet minister who was one of the restaurant's regular patrons. After tonight she would make very sure that their paths never crossed again!

She felt Morgan's breath feather warmly across her naked shoulder as he dipped his head to murmur, 'I was going to invite you to mine...' He clicked his tongue, laughter threading the dark, throaty purr as her haughty back stiffened, braced for whatever new outrage he was intent on perpetrating.

'Dear me, Duchess, didn't you know that our company maintains a permanent suite in this very hotel? When it's not occupied by visiting personnel or clients I sometimes use it myself if I don't want to bother driving home...'

He gave a mock yawn that raised taunting images of that long, hard, restless body twisting sensuously among the crisp white hotel sheets. 'And I certainly don't feel like bothering tonight. In fact, in the circumstances, it might be a good idea for me to move in for the duration. As you're a dutiful employee of the hotel dedicated to further its reputation and—er—*relations* with the public, I predict that you and I will be seeing a great deal of each other in the future...'

CHAPTER FOUR

'OVER my dead body!'

Four days later Claudia's shocked response to his silky taunt returned to haunt her.

She smiled grimly as she emerged from the shower and roughly towelled her gently steaming body. Her body was very definitely not dead; it vibrated with an unwelcome life at the very thought of *that man*! She had suspected he was a dangerous threat to her hard-won pride and precious equilibrium; now she knew he was...the memo laid out on her dressing-table confirmed it in black and white.

The tingling that enveloped her skin had more to do with the violence of her thoughts than the friction of the impatient drying and she cast a moody glance at her slender, rosy nakedness as she discarded the monogrammed white hotel towel and stalked from the small *en-suite* bathroom into the bedroom of her temporary residence. Damn that man—even in her thoughts she couldn't get away from him!

For the third night in a row Morgan Stone had evidently decided that he 'couldn't be bothered' to drive home and had stayed at the HarbourPoint. Not that Claudia had done anything more than glimpse him at a distance, but just the knowledge that he was somewhere around, effectively haunting her territory, made her uneasy. She had just started to feel comfortable in her new surroundings and now she had to brace herself every time she went out of the door of her room.

Still half inclined to think he had been baiting her with the threat of his unwelcome presence that first night,

Claudia had shut the door to her room sharply in his face and immediately got on the pone to the night telephonist, who was known to disdain the gossip that generally ran rife in the back of house and therefore could be trusted not to speculate on the reason for Claudia's interest. Joy Castle was a small, bird-like woman in her mid-thirties with an unexpected deep and sultry voice and she and Claudia had clicked instantly at the staff briefing at which they had been introduced.

'Joy, have you ever heard of Morgan Stone?'

'Honey, you can't live in Wellington and *not* hear about the man! I think that's his plan. He's the personification of brand-identification. Think Morgan Stone, think cars. Are you in the market for a Ferrari?'

Claudia shuddered. One of the pleasures of living-in was that you didn't need a car. 'On my salary? No, I just wondered—I haven't noticed any Stones on our permanent client list but I understand he has a permanent suite…' She trailed off and Joy obligingly filled the gap.

'Not him personally, his company—Morgan and Son—R5. Had it for about five years. Sends quite a bit of trade through the hotel, some of it real glamour stuff—you know, famous racing drivers, visiting celebrities, that sort of thing.'

Claudia's hear sank. R5. Although the hotel was fifteen storeys high it didn't actually possess a thirteenth floor, because many guests were superstitious about the number. Instead the hotel's gymnasium, sauna and spa were located on the thirteenth floor, and it was designated R, for recreation, on the lift controls and information sheets, rather than by its number. As well as the recreational facilities there was also a small restaurant located there, and five double-sized suites.

Morgan and Son. She had probably come across the name somewhere in the client lists during her orientation week at the HarbourPoint but had not registered it as significant. *Stone*, on the other hand, would have had all the alarm sirens blaring.

'I see... And does he often stay here himself?'

'I think he spends the odd night and sometimes, when he has a personal friend in residence there, he might stay a bit longer...'

'Personal friend? You mean—like...women...?'

There was a briefly startled silence, then a burst of more laughter. 'Claudia? Are you asking me if he uses his company's suite for assignations of an—er—illicit sexual nature?'

'No, of course not,' said Claudia hurriedly. 'I don't expect you to——'

'Relax, I was only teasing. I know you're not digging dirt just for the sake of it. He's single, anyway, so there's nothing actually illicit for him to hide. Some of them have been women, I guess, but the guy has class, if that's what's worrying you. He's got it but he doesn't have to flaunt it, if you know what I mean. He's not going to drag the hotel into disrepute——'

'No, of course not,' said Claudia hastily again, thinking wretchedly that she was more likely to do that than Morgan Stone. Although her ex-celebrity status was useful, it could also backfire if she wasn't cautious in her dealings with the Press. Fortunately she had begun building up a fairly good rapport with the Wellington media.

'Er—does he ring down for any regular special services?' she asked, trying belatedly to sound professional.

Joy wasn't fooled. 'Are we still on the same subject here?' came her droll rejoinder.

'*No!*' Ridiculously, Claudia could feel herself flushing at the gibe. From what Mark had said Morgan would be more likely to be paying women to stay away than vice versa... 'Joy——'

'Secretarial services, the masseur when he's worked out in the gym—he's a member of the health and fitness club—he sometimes runs conferences in the boardroom and has functions in the restaurant,' Joy listed cheerfully. 'I guess the only facility he *never* uses is the limo service,' she added with a chuckle. 'Anything else you want to know? I have a dozen calls on hold here.'

'Oh, no—thanks, Joy.' Claudia had hung up on the hasty lie. What she had learned already was disturbing enough. Morgan Stone was probably more familiar with the hotel than she was. It was obviously only sheer luck that she hadn't run into him before now. *Good* luck... which had evidently just run out!

Claudia pulled on her underwear now, and sat at her dressing-table to dry her hair quickly, trying to ignore the explosive memo lurking at the edge of her vision as she began to apply the make-up that presented the correct, confident image to the world.

Her dark colouring suited clear, vibrant colours and she had learned to use them skilfully to flatter her patrician features when she had lived with Chris. He had been surrounded by so many beautiful women that it had been a matter of sheer survival to learn how to look as attractive as possible at all times. Fortunately some friends who had been models had been willing to share a few tricks of the trade, but Claudia had found the constant emphasis on her appearance irksome. After Chris died Claudia had shovelled her make-up into a drawer and sold most of her expensive designer clothes with a sense of relief.

It was only when she went to work at Baron Hotels that she came to realise how valuable that rather tiresome training had been and how useful her image-enhancing skills could be if she astutely applied them to her job. As her self-confidence in her ability had grown she had actually found herself enjoying being on the other side

of the publicity fence, controlling the flow of information rather than being the victim of it!

Her make-up finished, Claudia dressed with inordinate care, donning the protective armour of her
uniform with meticulous attention to the lie of her collar
and the fastening of every button. She brushed her hair
until it crackled in protest, putting off the moment when
she would have to walk out of the door.

She looked at the cursory memo from Simon that had
been slipped under her door the previous evening.

Meeting in my office tomorrow morning at nine
sharp with Morgan Stone. He has a very exciting proposal to make!!

Claudia had blanched at the last sentence with its two
screaming exclamation marks, wondering for one insane
moment whether Morgan Stone intended to blackmail
her into marriage. Then reason had asserted itself and
she had gone to bed, tossing and turning all night, furious
with herself for the ludicrous assumption and torturing
herself with dread at what the morning might bring.

She took one last look at herself in the mirror and
almost groaned. In spite of the professional paint-job
her eyes looked slightly bruised through lack of sleep,
the tiny, distinctive downward droop at the outer corners
accentuated by tiredness, the gold flecks amid the brown
dulled by apprehension. Determinedly she pinned on a
smile. Not the warm, magical one which delighted her
friends but the cool curve which fended off all-comers.

Claudia's cubby-hole work-space was among a rabbit
warren of administration offices behind the ground-floor
reception area and distinctly unglamorous compared to
the outward trappings of the hotel. She went there first
to check her messages and run through her appoint-
ments for the day, fortifying her breakfastless state with
a strong black coffee before she walked along the windowless corridor to Simon's office.

She was deliberately early, hoping that she might be able to have a few quick words alone with him to prepare herself for whatever was going to blow up in her face, but as she approached his open door she could hear the low rumble of masculine voices, one of which made her toes curl in her navy shoes. Instead of her practical everyday pumps she was wearing heels as high as she dared. With her chin and eyes up, shoulders back, and a glittering smile stamped across her stiff mouth, she swept into Simon's office and promptly shattered the dignity of her entrance by almost stumbling over Morgan's briefcase set down squarely in the middle of the carpet.

'Sorry.' Morgan sounded more amused than apologetic as he rose from his chair and steadied her with an unwelcome hand on her arm, tucking the discreetly monogrammed case under the overhang of Simon's desk as she whipped her arm away and sat down in the second chair, clinging on to her composure by the skin of her teeth.

She crossed her legs, and then followed Morgan's narrowed gaze to discover that, by accident or unconscious design, her toe had tipped back until her long spike heel pointed directly at the man who had re-seated himself opposite.

'Armed and dangerous,' he murmured, and his gaze flickered up the full length of her leg and lingered for a moment on the outline of her hip in the immaculate narrow skirt before drifting up to her prim face— thinking to discompose her. She let her own gaze drift disdainfully over him. Now, if only she could find something to disdain!

For a man who wasn't very good-looking he knew how to look good, she allowed grudgingly. While Simon was attired in his usual dark suit, Morgan was dressed for the fresh and glorious summer day that already blazed outside the window. A linen sports jacket the colour of old roses worn over a plain white silk shirt, open at the neck, and white pleated linen trousers created a crisp elegance that was effortlessly casual. His shoes were white, too, canvas trainers that twitched as she looked at them.

'The curse of the second-hand car salesman,' he said, snatching her gaze back to his, adding, 'Flashy white shoes,' with a grin, knowing as well as she did that what he wore was far removed from the fancy polished leather implied by the popular cliché.

'And a personality to match,' Claudia was unable to resist adding.

'I didn't realise you two knew each other so well,' Simon said slowly, and Claudia opened her mouth to tell him that they didn't, then closed it again when she realised that it had been more of a warning than an idle comment. If she was going to trade insults with an important client Simon would want to know why.

'Oh, we share a few memories, don't we, Duchess?'

'Duchess?' Simon looked at Claudia's uncomfortable expression. 'Don't tell me you've even got a title tucked away in that glamorous past of yours?'

'It's just Mr Stone's little joke,' she said stiffly, making it clear she didn't find it very funny.

'You can drop the Mr, Claudia, I don't think Simon is fooled,' Morgan horrified her by saying. He leaned back, slewing sideways in his chair so that his body was angled towards hers, one arm casually draping over the back. 'Claudia and I knew each other a couple of years ago. In fact we had dinner together here just a few nights ago.'

'Oh, I see,' said Simon, who evidently didn't, but he was clever enough to pick up the undercurrents. 'Is there—is that going to be some kind of problem?' he asked delicately.

'Not for me. Claudia?'

She glared at her tormentor, trapped, knowing that he had created a totally spurious impression of their former relationship and realising that if she didn't act just as casually Simon would start getting a *very* wrong impression.

'Of course not.' Simmering at the gleam of triumph the appeared in the mocking blue eyes, she added unwisely, 'It's actually Morgan's *son* whom I was friendly with and the three of us were at dinner the other night. Morgan and I don't know each other at all, in fact have only met twice, very briefly——'

'But memorably,' said Morgan with a smooth mock-gallantry. 'Let's just settle for calling you a friend of the family, mmm? Which suits me well, because as you know, Simon, I like to do business on a relatively informal level. With Claudia I know exactly where I am.'

Claudia only wished she did. 'Perhaps one of you would like to tell me what this meeting is about,' she said sweetly, hoping to get the conversation back to less dangerous topics.

'Sure. Morgan, would you like a cup of coffee first? And you, Claudia? You don't look too bright this morning. Heavy date last night?'

Claudia managed a jokingly evasive answer to his teasing, uneasily aware of Morgan's sharpened glance. She was not going to confess that she was having trouble sleeping and thereby open herself up to more awkward questions.

'Now, Claudia, not being a local you may not know that Morgan is sponsoring this year's Sport Five Hundred; that's the annual five-hundred-kilometre sports car race around the streets of Wellington,' said Simon, dispensing with the stilted—on Claudia's part at least—small talk that had occupied them until his secretary brought in the coffee.

'In the past it's been sponsored by an oil company but this year Morgan and Son have taken over the major responsibility and naturally Morgan wants to make the most of the publicity that it offers his company. Since most of the overseas drivers are going to be staying here at the hotel, any publicity he generates is going to affect us and vice versa, so he's suggested that in order to prevent us doubling up on costs we link up to organise a week of race-orientated functions—rather like the floral festival ones you did last week. They were an enormous success by the way, Morgan, although the fact that you've asked for Claudia's input on this means I obviously don't have to sell her talents to you...'

'Quite.'

The dry one-word reply was such a marked contrast to Simon's expansive enthusiasm that Claudia felt herself blush. Fortunately Simon didn't seem to notice her discomfort.

'In fact, if this co-operative effort is a success we might well be able to get other businesses involved and turn it into an annual event—call it the automotive festival or something. What do you think, Claudia?' he urged. 'Excited at the idea?'

'Excited isn't the word for it,' she said weakly.

'Thrilled? Stirred? Stimulated? Hot and bothered?' offered Morgan slyly, reminding Claudia with this that his cleverness was not confined to selling cars. He had been bound for university before pride and circumstances intervened and she had a suspicion that he could tie her in verbal knots if he really brought that formidable intelligence to bear.

'I was thinking more along the lines of mildly interested,' she lied crisply. Terrified was an even better word!

'Really?' He leaned back in his chair, extending a leg so that he could thrust one hand casually in his pocket, the other holding his coffee-cup to his mouth. He looked the epitome of lazy relaxation but his eyes gave him away; they were like bullets of blue steel, firing silent questions at her. 'You don't sound like any PR person I've ever known. At this point a normal publicity agent would be swamping me with eager ideas...'

'Claudia's style is a little different,' Simon smiled, undismayed by the implied criticism. 'That's what makes her so good. She doesn't get carried away with the froth. She's cautious and ultra-practical—always looks at all the angles before she leaps. If she takes something on it's because she is certain she can build it into a success for the hotel. And she's never had a failure yet! Her track record is one of the reasons we were so glad she was transferred here——'

'Cautious? You do surprise me,' murmured Morgan, who hadn't taken his eyes off Claudia's stiff expression. 'I would have thought that Claudia was a bit of a firebrand, a creature of passion and impulse...'

Simon laughed. 'Claudia was right, you obviously *don't* know her very well. Rest assured, Morgan, that if she does decide to take this project under her wing you'll have her full and devoted attention.'

Morgan's crooked mouth curved faintly as a fleeting look of horror crossed Claudia's face at Simon's ill-chosen words.

'I'll look forward to that.'

Enough was enough. '*Decide*? Do you mean I actually have a choice?' Claudia asked sourly.

Simon looked a little puzzled by her sarcasm but it was Morgan who spoke.

'Of course,' he shrugged, 'if you don't think you're capable of handling it...'

She knew what he was doing. He was thrusting an adolescent challenge under her nose, thinking to manipulate her into accepting it. He must think her stupid.

'I *know* I'm capable,' she responded coolly, determined to prove to him that passion and impulse no longer held sway over her intellect. The last time she had allowed emotions to distort her reason had been two years ago and look where that had landed her! It had been the graduating lesson in what she now saw as her six-year course in maturity. Her expectations of life were greatly different from the expectations of that naïve, emotionally reckless girl who had considered the world well lost for love. 'I don't have to prove it to my ego by taking unacceptable risks——'

As soon as the word slipped out she regretted her choice, but it was too late.

'Risk? That's an interesting word for you to use.' His eyes were wide with cerulean innocence. 'What element of risk are you talking about? It's not as if I'm asking you to drive one of the cars yourself.'

Now Simon was definitely wary as he cleared his throat. 'Er—Morgan, did you know that Chris Nash——?'

'Yes, I'm fully aware of Claudia's background, but she's assured me that she's over the trauma of the crash that killed her lover,' Morgan cut across his tentative phrasing with a bluntness that took his challenge from merely provocative to utterly flagrant. 'If I didn't believe her I wouldn't be here. However, I don't believe that risk of a race accident is the hazard that Claudia is referring to...'

'Oh.'

Simon was rarely at a loss but this was clearly one of those rare moments.

Claudia looked helplessly from him to Morgan's coolly determined face, knowing she couldn't hold out any longer and still retain her dignity. She had known from the beginning that the deck was stacked against her but that knowledge didn't make conceding his victory any easier. She wondered exactly how to back down from her defensive position without looking more of a petulant fool than she did already.

'Well, I——'

'Perhaps if I took her away and explained my concept to her in detail—the way that I explained it to you—I might be able to alleviate her concerns...'

Once again Morgan had beaten her to the punch. Simon looked relieved.

'Good thinking, Morgan——'

'That won't be necessary,' said Claudia levelly, relieving him even more. She made herself smile brilliantly into her boss's puzzled eyes. 'I guess playing the devil's advocate isn't my scene. Actually I can see that there are some good possibilities here, for the whole of the Baron chain, not just the HarbourPoint. Why don't you let me work up some ideas——?'

'Us.'

'I beg your pardon?' She spoke to Morgan, carefully directing her gaze to the top button of his shirt.

'Not you—us. You and I.'

Still she refused to look at him as she tried to firmly put him in his place. 'Naturally I'll discuss your requirements with your advertising agency before I——'

'Not necessary. Their involvement will be in other areas. As I've already mentioned to Simon, I prefer to handle this particular promotion myself. *Personally*,' he added after a slight pause, so that she couldn't possibly misunderstand the threat.

He leaned abruptly forward so that his face slid into her deliberately narrowed field of vision, his features lit with a sardonic amusement that made her itch to slap it off. 'In this technological age I still think the personal touch has a lot to recommend it, don't you?'

'Oh, but surely your agency will want to be fully involved? I mean, many heads and all that...' said Claudia feebly, recoiling from the thought of exactly what his personal touch might entail. The more the merrier as far as she was concerned. If she could she would put the whole population of Wellington between herself and this man.

'Democracy is all very well but in this case I'm inclined to be autocratic,' he replied with the easy arrogance of absolute power. 'We only have two more months before the race so it'll be much more efficient for you to deal with me directly. I'm sure that between the two of us we can come up with some ideas that are sufficiently unusual to... excite your mild interest into something more profitable for us both...'

If Claudia had been feeling more like herself she might have laughed. He had a positive genius for wicked *double entendres*. But her sense of humour had been sorely tried these past few days and in Morgan Stone's company she was too often confronted with an unpredictable 'herself' she hardly recognised.

'Naturally I concede to your wishes as a client,' she bit out, unable to resist adding, 'Even though I happen to think that this time you're wrong.'

'Not client—*partner*,' he said, with silky satisfaction, holding out his hand as if he was the perfect gentleman. 'Do we have a deal?'

She took it, hiding her reluctance from Simon but not from the man across from her. Her eyes, which had been dulled with fatigue when she had walked into the room, glittered with repressed fury. She wouldn't have been surprised if he had tried to disconcert her even more by kissing her hand as he had when Mark introduced them, but his handshake was as firm and uncompromising as a promise. Her slim fingers were completely enwrapped by his, and the sensation of being trapped was stronger than ever. Claudia wondered uneasily just what kind of deal she had committed herself to as she withdrew, mentally and physically, from the hard physical reality of his confident grasp.

'Great!' Simon was eager to cement the alliance. 'I'll leave it up to you two to work out the details. You'll keep me fully posted, won't you, Claudia? We'll need to get head office approval since this will naturally reflect on our international image, but I can't see it being a difficulty, given that this is such a prestige event.'

'Meanwhile, I'll do as you suggest and bring Claudia up to date.' Morgan rose and turned towards her. 'Your office or mine?'

'I'm afraid I have a very full diary today,' Claudia was grateful to be able to inform him with perfect truth. She needed time to assimilate the unexpected turn of events, review her fast-diminishing options...

His blue eyes were mockingly sceptical as he towered over her. 'I'm a fairly busy man myself. Could you not perhaps spare just a minute or two for me now, out of your very full day...?'

Conscious of Simon's restless movement, Claudia capitulated. She might as well get this over and done with as soon as possible. If she did her job well, she might be able to keep their meetings to an absolute minimum.

'My first appointment isn't for another twenty minutes,' she allowed stiffly as she stood, determined to be crisp and businesslike. Even in her heels her eyes only came level with his chin—and a stubborn and pugnacious chin it was too, she recognised glumly. 'If you don't mind being rushed I suppose we could do enough groundwork for me to start drafting a plan.'

'Twenty minutes is ample time for what I have in mind,' he murmured blandly, sending shivers up her rigid spine as he followed her out of the doorway.

She stalked down the short hallway, conscious of Morgan prowling at her heels. As soon as he entered her small office it suddenly seemed claustrophobically smaller and Claudia hurriedly invited him to take a chair, hoping that the width of her desk would provide a bulwark against his intimidating aura of arrogant masculinity.

But as she brushed past him he caught her by the elbow with deceptively gentle fingers and her momentum swung her around to face him.

'Headache?'

He was so close that she could smell the heat of his skin, the scent of his maleness a confusing counterpoint to the softness of his deep voice. As she stared at him uncertainly one hard, square-tipped finger came up to stroke the crease between her brows and, before she could protest, his thumb traced the faint circles beneath her eyes. 'I know you didn't go out last night, so these must be due to something else. Conscience keep you awake?'

'I—no—as a matter of fact I slept like a baby,' she snapped furiously, trying not to tremble under his touch. Her damned conscience was so burdened; what did another lie matter? His answer, when it came, was devastating.

'Babies sometimes wake crying in the night,' he murmured with the bittersweet knowledgeability of parenthood, and his thumb moved delicately, as if wiping away imaginary tears from the darkened skin beneath her defiant eyes. 'Do you sometimes weep for your lost child, Claudia, in the still of the long, lonely nights?'

Claudia felt as if he had struck her to the heart. She jerked her head back from his disturbingly gentle touch, but his hand on her elbow restrained the violence of her recoil.

'You have no right——'

He answered her choked whisper with a whisper of his own. 'Who has more? Who else knows about your baby? We share a grief, Claudia, a secret sorrow. You haven't forgotten it any more than I have. You've just tucked it away, where other people can't see, can't hurt you with their casual compassion or curiosity. But you and I know it's there between us. And one day we're going to have to talk about it—to resolve the conflict——'

'No——' In her panic she tried to twist free, to goad him into revealing that his empathy was feigned, another trap to disable her reason.

He controlled her struggles easily, overpowering them simply by drawing her against his powerful body.

'Don't——' Her plea was muffled against his chest, her flushed forehead cradled in the warm hollow of his throat bared by his open collar.

'Then stop fighting yourself. I said one day...not today. We haven't established the ground rules, yet.'

She didn't dare try to interpret that cryptic remark. 'Let me go!'

'When you've calmed down. You're trembling and your heart is beating like a wild thing.'

She became acutely conscious of her breasts pressing against the hardness of his ribs and the thick, slow, steady beat of his own heart somewhere just below her ear. A strange and unwelcome tension entered her body, strengthening her fear. Wild. That was how he made her feel. Pursued and captured. And alarmingly safe.

One of his arms was wrapped around her waist, the other pressed vertically between her shoulder-blades, his firmly hand cupping the back of her skull. He enveloped her even more completely than he had on the dance-floor, holding her with an intimate familiarity that said a lot about him as a man and a disquieting amount about her as a woman. It was nearly three years since she had sheltered in such an intimate embrace and even then it had not been the tender cherishing she had needed when she had discovered she was pregnant. On the track or off, Chris was a man who had lived at top speed and even though she had loved him Claudia had sometimes felt left behind in the tumult of his whirlwind passions. Never had he had time in his headlong rush through life to just hold her, for no reason other than to be close. In his world hugs and kisses were casual currency between friends and acquaintances but if he tenderly put his arms around Claudia it was because the cameras were clicking, or as a prelude to lovemaking.

The dangerous drift to her thoughts pulled her up. She imagined what a stranger would think, walking into her office and seeing them now. She drew in a deep, uneven breath and her taste buds tingled at the salty male fragrance that filled the back of her throat in a suffocating rush of shocking awareness.

'I'm all right now,' she said, willing herself to sound calm, not to let him sense the subtle alteration in her resistance.

The hand that had been cupping her head slid around to tilt up her chin and he inspected her narrow face and wide, guilty brown eyes. His lashes screened the direction of his gaze as his lids drifted down but Claudia felt his look like a touch on her solemn mouth, and it lingered there until her lips began to hum with a curious warmth and a tide of colour rose up her throat.

He let her go then and sat down, an expression of blatant satisfaction on his face as he watched her scrambling retreat behind her desk, so much at odds with her former air of haughty command.

'I—— How do you know—that I didn't go out last night?' she blurted shakily, and then silently cursed herself for not returning immediately to business.

If anything, his satisfaction increased. 'I asked,' he said simply.

'Who? Why? How dare you spy on me?' Her voice was annoyingly breathless when she had intended it to sound firm and angry. When she got upset Claudia's vocal cords had an irritating habit of betraying her resolve, making her sound weak and kittenish when she wanted to roar like a lioness.

'Careful, Claudia, you know how irresistible I find a challenge,' he murmured provocatively. 'I dare because I care. You look far more human vibrating with outrage than you do dressed up in your air of cool indifference.

I told you we were going to see a lot of each other. You
should have believed me. From now on you will. I don't
lie.'

With effort Claudia managed not to cringe. 'And I've
already told you that I'm no threat to you and Mark.
As your spies no doubt told you, I haven't seen him
since that night at dinner—— '

The phone rang on her desk and Claudia snatched it
up with inordinate eagerness.

Her face froze when she heard the voice on the other
end. She swivelled her chair as far as it would go in the
arc of her desk, turning her head until only the sharp
purity of her profile was presented to the man sitting
opposite, her tone clipped and careful as she answered
in monosyllables.

'I know you've been looking for a nice flat. It's in a
perfect location for someone who doesn't have a car,
only a fifteen-minute bus-ride from the city. What do
you say? Why don't I pick you up at lunchtime and I'll
drive you out for a look—or after work this evening?
You'll need to snap it up if you want it because once a
place this good is advertised it'll go like a shot...'

Claudia suddenly realised why Mark's voice was re-
verberating oddly in her ears. Her head snapped around
and she saw Morgan's finger depressing the loud-speaker
button on the console of her telephone. There wasn't an
ounce of apology in his crackling command, 'Tell him
no.'

Claudia covered the receiver with her hand in a futile
attempt at protecting her privacy. 'I'll handle this myself,
if you don't mind.'

'I do mind. Your resistance appears to be nil where
my son is concerned—whatever he wants you seem to
give him and to hell with the consequences. Well, I'm
here now. You may not be able to deny him but I can.
Tell him that this time your answer is no. You won't
allow him to set you up in a convenient apartment...'

'How dare you——?'

'I warned you about saying that to me, Claudia,' Morgan said grimly. He leaned forward to speak into the console microphone. 'Sorry, Mark, the lady has other plans for her day—and for her future accommodation. She doesn't need any extra help. Have you told her yet that you're leaving for Italy next week? No?' He allowed his son the bare minimum of garbled response. 'Well, don't worry, I'll make sure that Claudia is kept fully informed of all your obligations.'

He delivered the final *coup de grâce* in a mercurial switch from brusque dismissal to sensuous warmth as he neatly confiscated the receiver from Claudia's nerveless hand and continued his outrageous monologue with more privacy than he had accorded her.

'What was that you said, Claudia, darling? Oh—she wants you to know that she's absolutely swamped with work herself, Mark, so she probably won't have time to see you again before you go. Oh, and by the way, don't expect me home tonight. I'm staying at the hotel. Yes—*again*. No, I don't think you do need to ask why; you've obviously leapt to all the right conclusions. Yes, of course I'll give her your love—as long as you realise that, while yours is necessarily platonic, mine is not. Goodbye, Mark.'

And with that he hung up.

And Claudia began to yell.

CHAPTER FIVE

'CAN I help you?'

Claudia's hand stilled on the glossy car roof and she turned to smile wryly at the nattily dressed young salesman who had approached her.

'I've never seen one of these before,' she murmured, still admiring the sloping lines of the aggressive two-door sports car.

'Beautiful, isn't she?' grinned the young man, not taking his eyes off Claudia. 'A Bricklin. Ford V8 engine with a top speed of 187 kph. Matches your nail-polish.'

Claudia was amused as much by his sharp eyes as by his flattery. She hadn't even noticed that the hot ginger was indeed the exact shade of her neatly manicured nails. 'You think I should buy it for cosmetic reasons?'

'It's as good a reason as any, but actually I don't think it's really your style.' He was young, barely more than twenty, and she suspected fairly new at his job.

'Oh?' Claudia raised her eyebrows, playing his game. Since she was the only person in the spacious marble showroom he was probably seeking to relieve the boredom of a slow day. Or perhaps her white ribbed cotton top, dressed up with a coral jacket and flared white cotton piqué skirt looked chic enough to seem expensive. The jaunty narrow-brimmed coral sunhat she had taken off as she entered probably added to the illusion of class. If she had been wearing her uniform instead of the 'civvies' she wore when she worked outside the hotel he would have placed her immediately as a non-customer. 'And what would you say *is* my style?'

'Something a little faster, maybe?' His eyes drifted south of the flirty hem of her short skirt and Claudia was acutely conscious of her bare legs. Thankfully they were tanned just enough to give the illusion of wearing tights. As with her arms, that pale tan had taken all summer to acquire through natural exposure to the elements. In spite of her dark colouring, Claudia's skin was so fair that she had years ago given up the drudgery of sunbathing.

'How about a Ferrari?' He ushered her over to the steel-grey, open-topped vehicle which occupied pride of place on a low ramp in the corner of the showroom.

She decided to tease him a little. 'A Ferrari is so awfully...*conventional*, don't you think? Middle-aged men drive Ferraris. Haven't you got anything a little more...flamboyant?'

She hid a smile at the expression of outrage that flitted across his face. He *was* young. And no doubt he, as any sensible young macho man would, lusted dreadfully after a Ferrari.

'A Porsche 911?'

She flicked her ginger fingers disdainfully. 'Too popular.'

A gleam in his eye told her she had aroused his fighting instincts and to disguise her laughter she turned her back.

'Ah! Now *that*! That is *definitely* me!' She wove her way around several other menacingly virile machines to stand beside a lustrous royal blue convertible, the stylish rear spoiler adding a wicked flip to its tail that thumbed a nose at all who trailed in its wake.

'A Corvette?' His sly delight as he hurried after her seemed to indicate that the reputation of Corvette women was not all that it should be.

'Here, hop in, try it out for size,' he said eagerly, opening the door, ignoring her hesitation as he whipped her fashionable leather document-case and hat out of her hand and virtually bustled her in behind the wheel.

The bucket seat conformed around Claudia's body as if it had been specially designed for it and the smoothness of the wheel beneath her fingers was such an unexpected pleasure that she didn't even notice that the swivel of her hips as she tucked in her legs had ruffled her skirt up around her thighs, or that the young man leaning on the door was fully appreciative of the distraction.

'It's a Greenwood. The only one of its kind in the country,' he told her smugly. 'And it's actually a bit faster than the Ferrari—not that you'd get much chance to test it around Wellington, unless you're in the Five Hundred.' He watched with interest as she settled more deeply into the blue leather upholstery and studied the impressive dashboard. He leaned across the top of the windscreen and grinned down at her. 'Will that be cash or a cheque, madam?'

Claudia returned his smile. The game was over. She hadn't done anything so light-heartedly foolish in ages. She sighed, running a caressing finger over the smooth curve of the steering-wheel. 'It really is gorgeous, isn't it? It's so...so...'

'Sexy is the word I think you're looking for.'

The young man's spine straightened as if he had been shot, his youthful cockiness deserting him. He stepped hurriedly back from the car, leaving Claudia staring directly into the shock of Morgan Stone's glorious eyes.

'Er—Mr Stone—I was just showing the lady the car——'

'And the lady was taking you for a ride,' Morgan interrupted his stammering with a faintly sardonic smile. 'Shame on you, Claudia, for taking advantage of Carl's youthful inexperience,' he chided, making her blush as if she were guilty of something more than mere frivolity. 'She probably knows a great deal more about cars like this than you do,' he told the chastened young man drily, taking possession of Claudia's hat and the document-case that doubled as a handbag and sending him on his way with a slight tilt of his head.

Claudia hurriedly swung her legs out of the car, only to find that Morgan's stance prevented her from standing up. She sat, skewed on the seat, glaring up at him.

'Well, *do* you think it's sexy?' Morgan asked, instantly making her think of the title of a song sung by Rod Stewart, one of her favourite artists. The answer, to both the mental and spoken question, was undoubtedly *yes* and an odd shiver of apprehension feathered along her nerves. This morning he was dressed with the same sophisticated elegance that he had shown that awful day in Auckland—a dark, double-breasted suit, white cotton shirt and muted olive-green silk tie with a scattered pattern of shell-like white fans. He looked a far cry from the casually dressed man who had firmly established himself as the bane of her life over the past week and Claudia suddenly felt vastly underdressed.

'It's very nice,' murmured Claudia, resenting her enforced submissive position.

'Nice?' The blue eyes narrowed in amusement, fine lines fanning out from the corners. 'That's like calling Fangio a good driver. You obviously have sinfully high standards. What kind of car did Nash drive off the track?'

As always, Claudia felt a jolt when he mentioned Chris's name with that unidentifiable edge that seemed to come into his voice when he referred to her former lover. 'A Boxer Berlinetta.'

'A man with taste.'

'Yes.' She wished she knew what was going on behind that deceptively tranquil expression because his eyes were certainly not calm, they were restless, penetrating, and his remark had an inflexion that didn't seem entirely complimentary. God forbid he should be able to read the confusion in her mind.

'I'm sorry I wasn't here when you arrived. I had an important meeting this morning, hence the formal attire.' He indicated his suit, for all the world as if he had divined the source of part of her discomfort. 'But I see that Carl has kept you amused.'

'He was only doing his job,' she felt bound to say defensively.

'Flirting with the female customers?'

'Isn't that part of the training?' she said tartly.

'True. May I help you up? That skirt must make that low-slung seat rather awkward to get out of without compromising your modesty.'

She would have liked to ignore his proffered hand haughtily but the mockery in his eyes made her all too aware of the truth of his statement. His ease of strength made her freshly conscious of his height and breadth when he pulled her upright. Instead of moving back from the door he had stayed where he was and her body rested full-length against his for a few disturbing seconds before he stepped away.

While she was still trying to decide whether the contact had been accidental or deliberate he handed her her possessions and placed a hand under her elbow, guiding her gently but very firmly across the marble floor towards an unmarked door in the windowless back wall of the showroom.

Expecting to be ushered into an office, Claudia was surprised to find herself blinking once more in the sunshine of a small brick courtyard shaded with a scattered planting of trees interspersed with several casually parked cars.

'I—thought we were going to your office.' So far all their preliminary meetings had been at the HarbourPoint where Claudia had at least had the illusion of being in control.

'It's just across the way.' Morgan indicated the striped awning sheltering a tinted glass door in the brick-fronted building on the other side of the courtyard.

Once there, however, Morgan paused only long enough to leaf through a stack of messages handed over by the sleek blonde behind an equally sleek polished wood reception desk and introduce Claudia to the grey-haired matron who was his personal secretary. She responded to Claudia's polite greeting with a warm smile and a look of frank curiosity that was transferred to her boss at his next statement.

'Claudia and I will be out for at least an hour, Irene.' After a sideways looks at the woman beside him he added softly, 'Or possibly two...'

'Where are you going?' Irene pre-empted Claudia's own startled curiosity.

'None of your business,' Morgan said pleasantly, and the older woman laughed.

'If it's not my business, then it's not business. If you're not back by five shall I send out a search party? You have a dinner engagement this evening.' It was evident that their relationship was tempered by a comfortable disrespect on both sides.

'Don't bother. If I'm not back by five I won't be worth rescuing,' he said drily.

'I thought you said we were meeting here.' Claudia found her voice, faintly hostile and defensive.

'And so we have,' he responded unarguably.

'But—I have all this information that you said you wanted.' She held up her document-case. 'You said we were going to discuss the choices for the celebrity lunches, and the chequered ball...'

Her idea for a ball the night after the race, the black and white theme taken from the colours of the checked flag that would greet the winner past the post, had been a hit with both Morgan and Simon.

'And so we will,' he confirmed, again in the indulgent manner of someone whose own plans were never flouted. 'But there's another priority. One I think you're going to appreciate. Irene—don't bother putting anyone through to the car-phone because I won't answer. No exceptions!'

'Well, if there's a crisis and the whole company comes crashing down around us—don't blame me!' his secretary said equably, inviting the sardonic reply,

'Let's get out of here, Claudia, before Irene really starts to nag.'

A few moments later Claudia was again being dazzled by the sunlit courtyard, and the car that Morgan was shoe-horning her into. It was a black left-hand drive convertible, small, blunt and uncompromisingly masculine from the steel mesh over the headlights and smooth bulge of the air intake on the hood to the chrome side-mufflers and roll bar behind the driver's seat.

'Is this yours?' she asked faintly as he shucked off his jacket and tossed it behind the driver's seat before sliding in behind the wheel.

'You mean mine personally, as opposed to being part of my stock? Yes, it is. I own several cars but the Cobra is my favourite.' The arrogance of wealth was in the casual statement of excess as he tossed her a few gratuitous titbits of information about his favoured vehicle. He flicked a mocking glance at her taut profile, adding provocatively when she did not respond, 'I have a taste for the unusual.'

'Are you trying to impress me, by any chance?' she countered, striving for a caustic amusement when every instinct was screaming for her to get out of the car and walk away. The hooded menace of the flared Cobra head on the marque suddenly seemed all too appropriate to the car's owner.

'Are you impressed?'

'Incredibly.' Her bored tone denied it.

He turned the key in the ignition and the engine snarled aggressively, almost drowning out his soft reply.

'Bitch.'

'Well, boys do tend to get rather tedious on the subject of their expensive toys,' Claudia said, her nails curving into the smooth leather sides of her document-case as she tried to concentrate on the conversation rather than the physical reality. She knew all about boys and their toys. She knew exactly what was going to happen.

And it did.

He was an excellent driver but she was sweating by the time they stopped at the first set of traffic-lights, with sufficient braking force to make the seatbelt tighten between her breasts.

'Still bored, Claudia?'

She stared rigidly out through the windscreen.

'Claudia?'

She didn't answer. She couldn't.

'Claudia?' He swore and reached out and turned her pale face towards him, swearing again when he saw her blank-eyed expression. The hand which had been firm on her jaw gentled to cup her cheek. 'Claudia? I'm sorry. Did I frighten you?'

She blinked, his hard features swimming into focus, his fingers warm against her cold cheek as he held her.

'That was a bloody juvenile thing for me to do, knowing what I do about you. I'm sorry.' Each word was slow and distinct, with a strong emphasis that penetrated her inertia. 'You were there at the track, weren't you, when Nash was killed?'

She blinked again, as if waking from a deep sleep, her eyes darkening as her pupils expanded to their natural daylight size, allowing her to see again, see his rigidly angry expression and know with some relief that it wasn't her he was angry with.

'I—yes.' She never spoke about that day. It was yet another painful memory pushed away out of sight. She shivered. When she didn't add anything else his fingers curled so that his knuckles brushed her rapidly warming skin.

'Do you still have nightmares?'

How did he know? She stared at him, wide-eyed. 'Sometimes. Not often…now.' The last said more firmly as she began to regain her shattered poise, rebuild the image of a woman who was in total control of herself and her destiny.

'Except when idiots like me reawaken them for you,' he said roughly. 'I'm sorry, Claudia.'

She had the feeling that the damned man would keep apologising until he had forced an acknowledgement from her so she shrugged. 'It's quite all right. You just took me by surprise, that's all. I mean, usually I'm OK if I have some indication before that I'm driving with——'

'A speed freak?' He cut across her polite attempt at forgiveness. 'I assure you I'm not usually so cavalier with the road code, especially in city traffic. My ego just eclipsed my better judgement for a few seconds.' He grimaced, aware of having told her that the car could accelerate to a hundred in just under four seconds. 'Is the car a problem for you? Would you rather have a closed sedan? Something less—er——'

'Boastful?' she offered with a stirring of annoyance, ducking her head away from the hand that was still caressing her cheek. Was he now going to treat her as if she were neurotic and feeble-hearted?

'Exposed, I was going to say.' The trace of uncertain humour in his tone gave a boost to her returning confidence. He might be in the driver's seat but he had just given her an indication that she was the one in control. 'Shall we got back and swap cars?'

'No. The Cobra is fine.' She suddenly became aware of the fact that the lights had turned green, and that there was a line of cars trapped behind them. 'As long as you drive it more sedately.'

His eyes flickered at the word. 'Perhaps you'd rather drive?' To her horror he shut down the engine and removed the keys from the ignition, holding them out to her.

She made no move to take them, staring at him in dismay as the car behind them began to toot impatiently. 'Morgan, we're holding up the traffic.'

'Perhaps you'd feel more relaxed if you were the one behind the wheel.' He dangled the keys at her and she hurriedly pushed his hand away.

'No, really, you drive. Morgan, they're tooting at us!' From being pale and clammy she was now flushed with embarrassment.

'Are you sure?' He seemed prepared to sit there all day, ignoring the cars that were pulling out around them. It was almost impossible to credit but he was actually *serious*.

'Yes, I'm sure,' she gritted. 'I wouldn't even know how to drive a car like this.'

He paused in the act of re-inserting the key. 'It's much the same as any high-powered car. What about Nash's Ferrari—didn't you drive that?'

Claudia gave a twisted smile. 'Are you kidding? Chris hated other people driving him, especially women. And he certainly wouldn't let me anywhere near his precious car on my own. If Chris wasn't around I took taxis everywhere.'

'Are you telling me that you didn't have a car of your own—that he wouldn't let you drive—and you let him get away with it?' he said, in tones of such incredulity that if she hadn't already been blushing she would have flushed deeply.

'I didn't need to drive,' she pointed out. 'We moved around so much that my having a car would have been a pretty pointless extravagance anyway. The class of hotel we stayed at always had limo services.' His expression of disapproval still hadn't faded and she added tartly, 'Some people do manage to survive without wheels, you know, especially in large cities with good public transport systems...'

'Usually people who can't afford the luxury. Which I gather wasn't a problem for you while Nash was alive...'

'I just didn't want to drive. OK? Is that a problem for you? Should I apologise or something? Is it an offence to your profession that someone shouldn't care whether they own a car or not? Do you want me to get out and walk? I may as well since it doesn't seem we're going to get anywhere with you in the driver's seat!'

'OK, OK, don't get hysterical, Duchess,' he had the gall to say, his eyes narrowing at the small outburst of temper that had transformed her former dazed inertia into energetic fury. 'See—I'm starting the car.'

'About time,' Claudia fumed, glaring at him as the engine growled impatiently. 'Well?' she demanded. 'What are you waiting for? Plant your foot, for goodness' sake!'

'I'd better wait for the light to go green, first,' he said meekly. 'I wouldn't like to break any more road rules.'

Claudia looked. In the interim the lights had turned back to red and so did she. They were back where they started. She almost exploded with the frustration of trying to keep calm.

'Plant my foot?' The baiting amusement was so overt in his voice that she refused to look at him. 'Not very sedate of you, Claudia.'

She crossed her arms over her chest in a very graphic demonstration of her state of mind.

'You're crushing your hat.'

She lifted her elbows. So she was. The rounded crown was sadly dented. Another fault to be laid at his door. She punched it out, watching him out of the corner of her eye. Morgan had twisted in his seat so that he was half lying against his door. His black hair was ruffled by the summer breeze,and his white shirt pulled tautly across his powerful shoulders. As she surreptitiously studied him he loosened the subdued tie and unbuttoned his collar, a picture of relaxation that highlighted her own nervous tension.

'Hadn't you better keep your eye on the lights? You don't want to miss a second set,' she said waspishly, arranging her hat meticulously on her knees.

'Oh, I don't know. I think it might be worth it.'

She looked at him sharply and was the recipient of a dazzling smile.

'I just learned more about you during one short traffic sequence than in all the previous hours we've spent fencing over ideas in your office,' he drawled.

During several meetings, alone and with Simon, over the past week Morgan had been so formidably businesslike that Claudia had almost shrugged off the unsettling feeling of waiting for the other shoe to drop. Following his unexpected lead, she had pushed aside the dangerous personal antagonism that had threatened to rage out of control and forced herself to view their brief professional partnership as a purely intellectual exercise.

Now, just when she had almost succeeded in believing what her cowardice wanted to be so *was* so, the other shoe—a hobnailed boot by the brutal sound of it—had been dropped with a resounding smash that brought all her doubts rushing back. How could she have allowed herself to imagine that he was anything but the ruthless manipulator he had proved himself in the past?

'I knew it was a good idea to get you out in the fresh air and sunshine,' he continued provocatively. 'And I hope that in the process you've also learned something about me?'

'That you're a bad driver?' she said, hoping to evade whatever uncomfortable observation he had up his sleeve.

He clicked his tongue, unoffended. 'That, whatever appearances might indicate, I don't wish to hurt or frighten you.'

He couldn't have chosen a remark better designed to frighten her. His seriousness, allied with that lazy air of predatory satisfaction, was totally disruptive.

'I see. That's why you've packed Mark off to Italy all of a sudden? Because you were afraid that he might *hurt* me...' she said sarcastically, still smarting over that humiliation.

'Mark packed himself of his own accord. Actually he's been wanting to visit the Ferrari works for some time. Wild horses wouldn't have stopped him accepting that invitation when it finally arrived—and even the omnipotent being you seem to think I am hasn't the clout to influence the personal schedules of car-builders in Milan and Turin. There *is* such a thing as coincidence...'

'Very convenient coincidence,' sneered Claudia, unwilling to underestimate him again.

'What a suspicious little soul you are, Claudia. Missing him already? He's only been gone twenty-four hours...'

'Look——'

'Excuse me, Mr Stone. Do you want me to call a mechanic? I've been parked down the road there and I notice you seem to be having some sort of problem getting your engine going.'

The policeman who was standing at the driver's door seemed torn between officiousness and admiration as he stared down at the car.

To her chagrin Claudia saw that the light facing them was green again, and that neither of them had noticed.

'The problem is with the passenger, not the car,' murmured Morgan wickedly, straightening in his seat as the officer transferred his gaze from the glossy coachwork to Claudia's pink face. 'And my engine is certainly going. In fact it's positively racing!'

'Oh!' The blue-uniformed bastion of male chauvinism grinned understandingly. 'I understand, sir. But I think you'd better get your show on the road. A great car, by the way.'

'Thanks. Incidentally, never call me a mechanic if you see me with a breakdown. I would never live it down with my people. I'm supposed to be a top mechanic myself. Any problem I have I can usually handle myself.'

The policeman grinned even wider, touching his helmet as he met Claudia's mortified gaze. 'So I see, Mr Stone. Have a good day, sir...ma'am.'

As they shot off with a smooth acceleration designed to please the admiringly envious policeman while allowing for Claudia's fears, she accused furiously, 'What did you say all that for? You know what he's going to think!'

'He was thinking it already. You were blushing so madly when he interrupted us that if this hadn't been a convertible he would have suspected we'd been making love instead of just talking.' He slid the gear-lever forward as he slowed down for a corner, taking in her expression as he checked her side for traffic. 'You're doing it again, you know. Are you thinking of the last time you made love in a car?'

'No, I was not!' she lied even more furiously.

'Don't tell me Chris didn't seek to combine the two great loves of his live on at least *one* occasion.' For the first time there seemed no trace of contempt in his use of her lover's name and, perversely, the teasing familiarity with which he referred to the past somehow removed the pain of remembrance. She had learned to be so defensive about her involvement with Chris that she had repressed all the good memories along with the bad.

'I think we should change the topic of conversation,' Claudia told him primly and he, as usual, refused to be guided by polite suggestion.

'I lost my virginity in a car.'

'How absolutely fascinating,' said Claudia frigidly.

'It was, rather. But extremely uncomfortable. It was a two-seater and the gear-stick got tangled up in my pants. My girlfriend was *supremely* impressed!'

In spite of herself Claudia laughed. And once she'd laughed it was impossible to regain the haughty aloofness she wore as a matter of course when Morgan was around.

'Was that——?' She stopped herself just in time. God forbid that she sound interested in anything about him.

'Mark's mother? Yes, it was. Marina was my first lover—although I, fortunately, wasn't hers. It was lucky that at least one of us knew what to do!'

Claudia was obscurely shocked. 'You mean, she'd . . . had other boyfriends?'

Morgan was amused by her attempted delicacy. 'She was eighteen; of course she'd had other boy-friends . . . but only one lover before me.'

Claudia's head buzzed with confusion at this intimate revelation. In a few brief sentences he had totally up-ended some of her most carefully nurtured prejudices. She hardly noticed that Morgan's gentle handling of the car had acquired an extra zip as they shot past the street façade of the HarbourPoint. 'She was *older* than you?'

'Two years older.' The corner of his mouth dipped. 'Not half the age-difference between you and Mark, but between teenagers an age-gap like that is scarcely significant. What's the matter, Claudia, doesn't that gel with your notion of the selfish, swaggering macho kid seducing a sweet young thing into abandoning her morals?'

'I wouldn't be that judgemental——' began Claudia lamely, conscious that she had thought something along those lines.

'In your position I don't suppose you can afford to throw stones,' he said with cruel perceptiveness, 'but people generally do seem to prefer making unflattering assumptions from the bare facts.'

'Yes ... well, you didn't do anything to dress up the bald facts you presented to me,' she pointed out. 'For an articulate man it seems to me you went out of your way to make it sound as if it had been all your fault.'

He shrugged as his hands shifted lazily on the wheel. 'In a way it was. Although Marina may have been sexually more mature than I, I was the more so emotionally. I adjusted far more quickly to the implications of her...pregnancy than she did. I'd have been quite happy to accord her sole responsibility for contraception therefore I couldn't quibble at accepting my share of responsibility for its failure.' His hesitation over the word *pregnancy* would have been unnoticeable to the average listener, but to Claudia it spoke of a sensitivity to which she was acutely attuned.

'Did it ever occur to you——?' She broke off, scarcely believing what she had been about to ask.

Again he seemed to be able to catch her thoughts before she had even voiced them.

'That she had deliberately got herself pregnant in order to marry me? Yes, it occurred to me, especially when she pressured me to accept the financial help of my family, but with the wisdom and hindsight of experience I can say no. She was too devastated by it all for it to have been premeditated. And she didn't really want to be married any more than she wanted to have the baby, but not having it or giving it up for adoption was incompatible with her upbringing ... or mine for that matter.'

There was so little bitterness in his words that Claudia wondered whether, for all the evidence to the contrary, he had loved the girl for whom he had altered the whole course of his young life. 'How did she die?'

A tiny pause. 'In a car accident.'

Claudia sucked in a shaky breath at the certain knowledge of the sudden impact of his loss. 'Oh, I'm sorry.'

'So am I. It was such a waste. She was young—only twenty-three—and full of life, just starting back at university on the degree course that she had forfeited when she got pregnant. I wasn't driving—I wasn't even in the car.'

That last, abrupt comment spoke volumes. 'I didn't ask,' she said huskily.

'But you were wondering.'

There was a tension in the hands gripping the wheel that she could not mistake. 'As a matter of fact, I wasn't. You're a very good driver.'

His pale knuckles relaxed. 'You didn't think that ten minutes ago,' he murmured a trifle sardonically.

'There's a big difference between speed and recklessness. Even *I* speed sometimes.'

Her attempt at humour fell flat as he shot her a speculative look. 'So you *do* drive.'

'Of course. I'm not a complete neurotic.'

'Just a sometime one?' His humour reinflated in direct proportion to hers. 'Was Chris reckless when he drove?'

'On the open road, yes. Never when he was working. On the track he was fast but he was cool and calculating; he never broke the rules. When he drove for pleasure he made his own rules—he literally was without fear. He carried his fate around with him, you see. He knew that if he was going to get killed it would be on the track, so off it he considered himself invincible.'

'A tough attitude to live with,' was the only comment. And then, 'Was it he who didn't see any future in your relationship—or you who was frightened of it?'

This time he had gone too far. Claudia recoiled mentally from the consequences of her impulsive confidence, pushing back the silky strands of hair that had whipped across her face as she prepared a deadly, conversation-stopping reply. As she opened her mouth Morgan grunted with satisfaction and pulled into the kerb, neatly slotting himself in behind a car that was pulling out from the solid line of parked vehicles that lined both sides of Oriental Parade.

'What are we doing here? Where are we going?' she demanded belatedly.

'I thought you were never going to ask,' he replied blandly. 'Considering your somewhat savage mistrust of my motives you've been amazingly trusting. In this case your trust is about to be justified. We're going home...'

CHAPTER SIX

'IT'S totally out of the question!'

Claudia stood in the middle of the elegantly furnished apartment, hands on hips, her eyes blazing at the man lounging against the back of the wide cream leather couch.

Morgan studied her calmly. 'Why? It seems like the perfect solution to me. You said you were looking for a place to live. Why not here?' He pushed himself away from the couch and strolled across to the sliding glass door which opened out on to a small balcony. 'It's free, it's private, it has a great view, and Oriental Bay is incredibly convenient to the city—in summer you'll be able to walk to work—I know you like walking because Simon said it was your enthusiasm for exploring the city on foot that led to the hotel's producing a "sightseers' fitness course" brochure.' He opened the door and stepped out on the balcony, leaning over the rail. 'Look, you can even see the HarbourPoint from here.'

Claudia didn't move. None of the reasons made a blind bit of difference as far as she was concerned.

'I'm not interested. Can we get back to business now?'

He walked back towards her, the sun streaming in the windows behind him forming a nimbus of light around his white shirt and concealing his expression from her.

'Why, Claudia? You didn't instantly turn your back on Mark's offer to help you find a flat. Consider this reparation for my losing you the opportunity of that one.'

'That was different,' muttered Claudia, summoning the wits which had been scattered the moment Morgan had finished showing her around the top-floor water-

front apartment and told her that it was hers. The fact
that he had *told* her rather than offered or asked had
got her back up for a start.

'Oh? In what way?'

'It wasn't *his* apartment——' she began defensively.

'And this isn't mine.'

'Your company's, then——'

'Not that, either. Peter is simply a friend who just
happens also to work for me,' Morgan cut in mildly. 'He
would be very offended at your suggestion that he doesn't
own his own home. He's spending the next four months
in Germany and the house-sitting arrangement he had
with a student fell through just before he left. He doesn't
want to risk leaving the place empty and asked if I would
do him the favour of finding someone trustworthy to
look after the place for him...'

'And you, of course, thought immediately of me!'
Claudia said sarcastically. 'Since when have you
honoured me with your trust...?'

'Is that how you see my trust, Claudia? As an
honour?' he said silkily, approaching closer, and she
panicked, backing away until the arm of the couch
stopped her.

'I—anyway, I'm looking for a permanent place——'
she stammered hastily.

'Then consider this a stepping stone. It'll take the
pressure off while you look around.' He picked up a
heavy blown-glass *objet d'art* that sat on the sideboard
at his elbow and turned it over in his hands, his eyes
intent on the way the light was refracting through it as
he murmured slyly,

'Remember, with Mark away and the Five Hundred
coming up I'll probably be staying at the hotel more often
than ever. So if you want to keep up your avoidance of
me in your off-duty hours you'll have a better chance
here than at the hotel. Here you don't have to treat me
with the deference due to a valued client. Here you don't

have to pretend. Here the only way I can see you is by
your own personal invitation...'

She was being shamelessly manipulated, she knew, but
that didn't change the truth of what he said. Suddenly
she could see advantages where before only unwelcome
complications had loomed. It was on the tip of her
tongue to deny that she had been trying to avoid him at
all but she sensed to do that would tempt fate indeed.

'I—don't know,' she prevaricated, looking around. It
was a lovely apartment, one of only four in the irregu-
larly shaped building a stone's throw from the water's
edge. The cliché made her smile. She knew one Stone
whose arrogance might benefit from the occasional
dunking!

'You *do* want it...so take it!' he said, replacing the
glass sculpture with a confident smile that interpreted
the softening curl of her mouth as a victory, which she
wasn't prepared to give him so easily.

'That's your philosophy in life, is it?' she said tartly.

'As long as you pay for what you take,' he shrugged.

'But you said this apartment was free,' she pointed
out sweetly. 'In fact, if I'm house-sitting—providing a
service—shouldn't *you* be paying *me*?'

'In cash or in kind?' he countered easily. 'Name your
price, Claudia.'

That so closely echoed his bitter offer of two years
ago that she was shaken by a stormy conflict of emotion.
'You already paid my price, remember?' she said unwisely, turning away.

He stopped her with a mere touch; a single finger on
her coral sleeve that burned through to her bare skin
beneath, spinning her around as if he had caught her by
the throat.

'I rather thought it was you who had done the paying
last time,' he said gravely. 'No amount of compensation
can replace a life. Consider this favour I do Peter just
part of the debt I owe you.'

'You don't owe me anything,' Claudia said desperately, wanting to run and hide from the brooding blue gaze. 'The past is just that, the past—over and done with! You've told me how sorry you were. So am I. Let's leave it at that.'

'"Words pay no debts",' he quoted softly. 'Shakespeare had the right of it. What I owe you can't be settled in words, nor with money.' She made the mistake of looking at him then, and he added, eyes glittering with a grim purpose, 'And no, I won't leave it. I *can't*...' The words had the ring almost of a vow and Claudia immediately began to panic again.

'Look, I'm taking the apartment,' she said. 'I'm very grateful and——'

'I don't want your gratitude——'

'Then what *do* you want?' she blurted out angrily. 'Why are you doing this to me? For revenge——?' She bit her lip as his gaze sharpened.

'*Revenge*? Why should I want revenge? What have *you* done to *me* that you think I'd need to seek retribution?'

There was an awful silence during which Claudia was sure her anguished uncertainty was written clearly on her pale face. *Now*. Tell him now, her brain urged. Here is the perfect opportunity to clear the slate. To start again...or finish it forever...

'I—I——' As she struggled for the words that would totally destroy any possibility of respect or friendship or anything else between them, he continued thoughtfully,

'What is it that I *am* doing to you, by the way? Besides providing you with a fine professional opportunity to prove yourself in a new job, of course, and helping you find accommodation in a strange town, and asking for forgiveness for mistakes—past and present. What exactly is it that makes it so difficult for you to accept anything from me...?'

He hadn't moved any closer but suddenly she felt crowded. 'Morgan——'

'Is it this, Claudia . . . ?'

This wasn't just a finger. This time his whole hand restrained her nervous shying, sliding under her unbuttoned jacket and around her slender waist, hooking her startled body into the circle of his arms.

'Isn't this what you're afraid of, Duchess?'

His parted mouth came down on hers, damming the cry of protest in her arched throat, sending a dazzling bolt of fearful excitement shearing through her consciousness. After the first instant of quivering shock it was like being enveloped in a slither of hot, wet silk that bound her, stroked her, wrapping around her senses, entangling her in inescapably erotic knots.

The world went black as she closed her eyes, shutting out the deliciously terrifying sight of Morgan's blue eyes a breath away from hers, blazing with a carnal intensity that was matched by the sensual movements of his mouth. It was a mistake. Now there was nothing to distract her from the pure intoxication of her tactile senses.

With the extent of her vulnerability screaming in her mind she tried to shut him out, but he would have none of it, nipping softly at her lower lip until she allowed him precious access again, dominating her with his lips and teeth and tongue in a way that frightened and exalted her. That battle won, he smoothly adjusted his grip on her torso, his fingers splaying out around her waist to overlap at her back, his thumbs digging into the soft ribbed cotton just below the weight of her breasts, moving back and forth in a sensuous precursor to the caress to come. In spite of her confusion Claudia responded like a flower to the sun, unfolding to the warmth of half-forgotten feelings and sensations that had for too long been associated with the accompanying pain of emptiness and loss.

Unknowingly she rose on to her toes, flexing her spine, faintly arching and twisting her hips, the white piqué skirt flaring across the dark fabric of Morgan's trousers as she sought to assuage the empty ache aroused by his sudden assault. She felt a thick ridge of flesh compress briefly under her dragging hipbone and then spring bluntly forward into the hollow cup of her pelvic girdle, realisation of what it was bursting upon her comprehension too overwhelmingly for her to pretend ignorance. Her eyes flew open. His were still there, brooding in wait for her, swamping her field of vision in a hot blue haze, watching her arrive at the shocking knowledge of what she was doing to him ... and he to her.

'No——' Her tiny breath of denial died on his tongue as it curled over hers in a gesture that was both intimately protective and provocatively sensual. She moved her head and he let her go, but only in order to feast on the frantic pulse beneath her ear, his mouth cascading gently down the exposed nerves of her throat to settle moistly in the vulnerable pool of her collarbone, licking at the clamour of blood under her skin.

'Yes...' His thumbs pressed upward, compressing her swollen flesh in a sensual parody of the way her hip had stroked his, then releasing it, only to press again, moving her breasts rhythmically against the lacy cups of her bra so that the tips stiffened with the delicately judged friction.

'Morgan...' Her hands clutched at his shirt-front, seeking to ground herself in the solid reality of his presence, to warn her dwindling resistance that this wasn't simply a reckless figment of her sinful imagination.

'Yes...' He wasn't replying to her weak plea, but fervently approving the tremors of delight he could feel rippling through the supple arch of her body. His thighs moved, urging her unsteady legs softly across the carpet until her bottom hit the firm rounded arm of the couch. His languid momentum carried him further as he rode up over her thighs, straddling them with his, bending her against the couch and the brace of his hands as his mouth nuzzled at the white cotton over her breasts.

Claudia found herself blinking at the ceiling, dazed at the speed and intensity of the conflagration in her senses, her limbs weighted by an unprecedented pleasure. If this was truly happening surely it wouldn't feel so— so... incredibly good... so *right*? And if it was a dream it was the most erotic one she had ever had...

Her hand slid up over his loosened collar to sink into the frosted darkness of his hair at the back of his head, her fingers tightening in instinctive protest among the short, soft strands as she felt his movements momentarily still. Then he was in satisfying motion again, rubbing the hard angles of his face against the stretched cotton in a deliberately explicit gesture of possessiveness that made her say his name again, this time in a whisper of bewildered need.

He uttered a thick growl of satisfaction, dragging up her ribbed top and moving his mouth over the creamy curves exposed by her low-cut bra. Across the bare slope of hill and provocatively perfumed valley he strung a line of luxuriant, biting kisses that melted like hot honey down over her sensitive flesh, drenching her with a sweetness that seeped into the very heart of her being. Now she had both hands in his hair, urging him fiercely to her pleasure, aching for him to touch the lace that he was so assiduously avoiding, the passionate restraint of his tender assault both a joyful revelation and a searing frustration.

Not until she felt the fingers slowly easing up her flank, catching the hem of her skirt and pushing it high over her captured thighs did she feel the trickling return of her former fears.

She murmured, struggling to surface from her sensual stupor, and he soothed her by at last seeking one of the rigid peaks sheltering behind the seams of her bra, taking it between his teeth and biting, firmly. Wanton desire exploded violently in the pleasure centres of her brain, obliterating her returning reason. Her head fell back in erotic shock as in the same moment he shifted the hand under her skirt gently between their bodies and touched the secret V that sheltered her femininity. It was a light, sliding touch, one fingertip barely intruding between the silky compression of her inner thighs, clamped together between his powerful knees, but combined with the stinging tug on her nipple the explicit delicacy of that warm fingertip curling against the clinging film of her panties was every bit as shattering as his full possession would have been.

Claudia uttered a frantic cry, convulsing helplessly, blind and deaf to Morgan's muttered curse as his head jerked up and both arms whipped tightly around her to secure her shuddering length firmly against his. As she continued to be racked by shivering contractions he lifted one thigh, roughly pushing it between hers, seeking to ease the painfully exquisite need that he could see expressed in her tautly stretched body, her wildly flushed face and lustrous golden eyes.

With a greedy fascination he watched as the woman in his arms peaked and gradually quieted. His head pounded with hot-blooded triumph, mingled with a savage sense of possessiveness and almost angry envy of the uninhibited bliss she had stolen from what he had only intended to be a little light-hearted lovemaking.

Any minute now Claudia was going to realise what had happened and it was going to take some very skilful handling on his part to persuade her that her newly revealed vulnerability to him was not something he was going to take ruthless advantage of...even if he was!

Claudia didn't want to lift her head from his chest but she knew she was going to have to face him some time. She couldn't hide her shame forever.

She forced herself to stand stiffly straight within his arms, silently indicating that she no longer needed his support, and slowly raised her chin, mentally cringing at the prospect of meeting his knowing gaze.

But instead of smug or leering satisfaction she found Morgan's expression sombre and curiously gentle. That only made her feel worse. He was probably thunderstruck... disgusted, even. *She* certainly was! She sought desperately for an explanation for her scandalous display and realised there was none. Her flushed face paled, then flushed again. There was no graceful way out of this humiliating embrace, she thought miserably. Whatever she said he was going to think that he had just proved she was every bit the promiscuous tramp he had always suspected her of being!

The silence stretched unbearably. There was no use waiting for him to get her off the hook. It seemed he was content to stand there forever, waiting for her to speak. What could she say that might bring some semblance of normality to this horribly abnormal situation? She scrabbled for a neutral topic, something that might allow her to back off with at least the semblance of her pride intact.

'Er——' She cleared her throat and made a half-hearted shuffle with her shoulders and to her surprise Morgan let her go. She moved an uncertain step away and watched him push his hands into his trouser pockets, bunching out the dark, pleated fabric. Definitely a man waiting for something. Say something, Claudia—*any-thing*—to demonstrate that you aren't the frenzied madwoman of a few moments ago...

'I—you—are you really a qualified mechanic?' He looked at her incredulously and she continued doggedly, 'I mean, you told that policeman that you fixed cars.

Did—did you do the usual apprenticeship...?' Oh, God, this was terrible. She sounded like a prim spinster at a tea-party making polite conversation with a stranger!

His burst of laughter confirmed the absurdity of her choice and she blushed even more fierily as he finally calmed down enough to shake his head.

'Is that a criticism, Duchess? Are you trying to tell me in a roundabout way that my performance just now was disappointingly mechanical?'

Performance? The word implied a detachment on his part that was an insult and his faint emphasis on *disappointingly* made a pointed mockery of any denial she might offer. He knew very well that the last thing she had been was disappointed!

He was still laughing and anger began to replace her crippling embarrassment. But in the next instant he whipped the ground from under her by saying with a warm chuckle, 'I can assure you, Claudia, that the mechanics of what we were doing was the very last thing on my mind. In fact I don't think my brain was engaged at all; I was operating purely on instinct. All I could think was how incredibly delicious you tasted and how eager you were for my touch, how generously responsive you were...'

She knew it! 'I am *not* promiscuous!' she told him raggedly.

'I never said you were,' he said, his face again adopting that dangerously inviting gentleness. He had no right to stand there looking so...cool and untouched when Claudia was a welter of anguished self-disgust.

Well, not precisely cool, she corrected herself. There was a certain indefinable, smouldering heat in those innocently sky-blue eyes. And not entirely untouched, either. His mouth was reddened and faintly swollen, its usual crooked narrow line looking surprisingly lush and sultry, and his closely groomed hair was ruffled unevenly. He took his hands out of his pockets as she frowned suspiciously at him, and she discovered what his gesture had originally been designed to hide when the bunched material relaxed over an explicit tautness.

Too late, she snatched her eyes back to his face.

'And nor, I might add, am I,' he murmured, confirming her discovery with a ruefully frank reference to his continued state of sexual readiness, 'just because I find being with you intensely arousing. What happened naturally happens between men and women. The survival of the entire species depends on it...'

'But I—you——' She was confused by his apparent benevolence. Could it be that he really didn't realise exactly what *had* happened to her alone—had he been too caught up in his own pleasure to realise the extent of hers?

He dashed her faint hope with a smile. 'You just outpaced me a little this time, Claudia. Nothing to look so embarrassed about. I'm very flattered that you trusted me enough to let yourself go.'

This time? Her heart shuddered at the casual tossing down of the flagrant gauntlet of his intent. As to letting it happen—he flattered her by assuming that she had had any control whatsoever over her responses.

'But I don't—I mean I didn't mean...it all was a mistake...' she said frantically. 'I don't usually—I mean, I've never—oh, *God*!' With a moan she covered her embarrassed face with her hands.

'Never gone so far so fast? Or never had an orgasm before?'

'*Morgan*!' She was sure that by now she was pink all over.

'I'm sorry if it embarrasses you to talk about it, Claudia, but not sorry enough to regret what we did. I enjoyed overloading you with pleasure, so much so that I think it could become very quickly addictive...'

She peeped out between her fingers to see if he was teasing and almost groaned out loud at the expression on his face. *Now* he was looking smug and self-satisfied. And, instead of shaming her as she thought it would, the swaggering of his male ego made her feel shockingly aware of the depths of her own sensuality.

He took her wrists and pulled her hands away from her face. 'There's no point in trying to hide any longer from the attraction between us, Claudia,' he told her gravely. 'It's just been proven beyond a doubt. You want me. I want you. Sexually we're exquisitely compatible. That accepted we should discuss the other possibilities available in our relationship...'

Claudia stopped trying to pull her wrists away, subduing a traitorous pang of disappointment as her eyes flicked momentarily down below his waist and skated nervously away. 'You mean you don't——' She broke off and he took pity on her confusion.

'Want to take you into the bedroom right now and confirm that compatibility to both our satisfaction? You don't know how badly.' He rolled his shoulders and shuddered slightly in a graphic attempt to shake off the tension in his big body. 'But I can wait. I didn't bring you here to seduce you. At least not to the point where you could later claim that I swept you off your feet without allowing you to weigh the consequences of your actions. I know that you consider yourself a cautious woman. For the moment I'm willing to respect that caution. Hungry?'

'What?'

'It's lunchtime.' He cocked her a wicked grin. 'Doesn't time fly when you're having fun?'

She managed a very shaky smile. 'If that was fun why do I feel so battered and bruised?'

'I could give you a very indecent answer to that but instead I'll undertake to feed you lunch while we talk about the contents of that briefcase you brandished at me earlier.'

'I—I'll need to freshen up,' said Claudia, discon-
certed by his cheerful change of subject and thinking
that if they were going to a public restaurant it would
be better for her reputation if she didn't look as if she
had just climbed out of bed with her escort.

But when she emerged from the bathroom it was to
find Morgan setting the small table on the sunny balcony
with food from a woven hamper that lay open at his
feet.

'Where did that come from?' she demanded suspiciously, having been shown around an empty kitchen
earlier. No takeaway delicatessen delivered that fast!

'The boot of my car.'

'Do you always carry around emergency hampers?'
She approached warily to check the mouth-watering in-
gredients he was placing on the white tablecloth.
'HarbourPoint deluxe hampers at that!' She recognised
the labels from the hotel brochure.

'Only when I'm attempting to persuade a highly dis-
cerning lady to like me,' he said, waiting until she was
seated on one of the wrought-iron chairs before he sat
himself.

'Is it really necessary that I like you?' said Claudia
stiffly, not sure how to view the fresh evidence that he
had had far more planned for this day than he initially
let on.

'Essential,' he said simply. 'No matter how sublime
the sex, I can't make love to a woman who doesn't appreciate my mind as well as my body. You'd never respect me afterwards.

'Now, stop trying to provoke me and eat. And tell me,
have you decided on anyone in particular to design the
invitations for the ball? I know of a very talented young
graphic artist you might like to consider. And what would
you say to one of the world's leading racing drivers and
the head of a famous champagne house as celebrity
speakers for starters?'

CHAPTER SEVEN

MORGAN poured the last of the bubbling wine into her long-stemmed glass and Claudia twirled it between her fingers, wondering how much of the bottle she had drunk but too relaxed to care. She knew by now that Morgan had no need to seduce a woman with alcohol. He did quite well without any artificial aids!

Her attitude was very different from what it had been two weeks ago, when they had sat together on the balcony of the Oriental Bay apartment she had eyed the wine that Morgan had produced from a chilled compartment of his hamper with suspicion and disfavour.

Both then and since that suspicion had proved unfounded.

Then, he had deftly eased her over the barrier of her mortification by plunging into a lively debate over the ideas that she had produced for his approval, subtly challenging her on a number of points so that she was forced to concentrate on her arguments rather than the intimate submission that he had just extracted from her.

Even so, she hadn't quite been able to conquer the flustered leap of her heart when her hand had inadvertently brushed his while pointing out a paragraph on her sheaf of papers, or when she had looked up to catch him studying her with a narrow-eyed speculation that she knew had nothing to do with the subject in hand.

Today, he had used that same earnest concentration on detail successfully to take her mind off the fact that this time the balcony was his and the lunch prepared, not by the hotel kitchen, but by his housekeeper.

The meal had been light and delicious, the panoramic view from his clifftop home glorious and business satisfactorily disposed of in a thoroughly professional fashion. In fact, Claudia was feeling confident enough to feel that she could handle almost anything at the moment—even Morgan Stone.

The promotion centred around the race was shaping up nicely, a fact which, she was willing to admit, had a lot to do with Morgan's persistent involvement. Although he was ruthlessly efficient in his business dealings, demanding a high standard of performance from those who worked with and for him, he was equally demanding of himself. In her first-hand observance of his business acumen Claudia had come to see that part of the strength of his company was his own dedication to excellence coupled with a personal charisma that evoked the loyalty of his employees even when they were at loggerheads with him.

Only on two occasions had she been given a glimpse of the dogmatic autocrat that Mark had so resented as a teenager. Both times had been at his office when Morgan had lost his temper over what Claudia had thought were relatively trivial matters but which he seemed to see as an intolerable attempt to pre-empt his authority.

She had got the strong impression that Morgan actually *enjoyed* the shouting and pacing and banging things around on his desk like a bad-tempered boy. Certainly after both incidents he had appeared cheerfully refreshed and invigorated, as if his outburst had shed some of the internal tension that seemed part and parcel of his complex personality. And, from the wry grin she had received from the first chastened victim as he had slunk out of the door, she thought the employees who knew him well had learned to take the odd tantrum in their stride.

She, too, had learned a valuable lesson. If you stood up to Morgan you had a far better chance of getting him to listen to you than if you tried to appease him by making excuses, however justified.

Intrigued as she was by these insights into his character, Claudia had stuck firmly to her resolution not to allow her personal curiosity dangerous rein. She had never invited him back to her new apartment—not even to the small housewarming she had held—and she never accepted an invitation from him without first satisfying herself that it was solely business-related.

Still, that criterion had proved amazingly flexible and in this past fortnight Morgan had managed to produce an impeccable reason for her company almost every second day. In the process he had contrived to introduce her to a considerable number of influential Wellingtonians who would be useful contacts, not only for the current project, but for future ones as well. He had even managed to get her invited to two embassy cocktail parties which she would have been a fool to refuse, even if this had meant accepting Morgan as her escort. There she had encountered a Morgan she had never seen before—urbane, almost courtly in the politeness that sheathed his normally blunt self, and on first-name terms with many of the high-level political movers and shakers they encountered.

Shortly afterwards Simon had complimented her on her cleverness in gaining such a swift entrée to the cream of Wellington society and on the second Friday of what Claudia wryly thought of her as her unholy alliance he had passed on the information that head office was so impressed with her plans that it wanted to increase the hotel's involvement by sponsoring one of the cars, if possible.

That, of course, had required yet another discussion with Morgan but he had been unable to fit it into his schedule and had suggested the next day. Claudia had been too pleased with the prospect of a new feather in her cap to balk when he had added that his weekends were normally inviolate but that, providing he didn't have to come into the business district, he was willing to compromise. He had all the extensive race files at home on his personal computer, including those individuals still seeking whole or partial sponsorship, and she was welcome to take advantage of them.

Nervously aware that she was stretching her self-imposed rules to suit the dictates of her disobedient curiosity, Claudia had agreed, but had borrowed one of the hotel cars so that she had the security of knowing that she could leave whenever she wanted.

'Shall I crack open another bottle?'

Claudia surfaced from her meandering thoughts and realised that her glass was empty again.

'We're not celebrating anything are we?'

It was a leading question, which Morgan wisely declined to follow to its tempting conclusion. He raised his glass to her.

'Only the prospect of another long, slothful summer weekend. Would you believe I used to work all the hours God made? That was before I realised that I was slowly petrifying in the ivory tower of my own self-importance. I was losing touch with the simple pleasures of life. I was growing old while still trapped in the selfish ambitions of my youth—to have enough money and power to do whatever the hell I wanted. I just never stopped long enough to figure out exactly what it was I *did* want so desperately.'

'You still seem to be fairly confident of your own self-importance,' Claudia was unable to resist commenting, although the acerbic tone was tempered by her hesitant question, 'And when you did figure it out—what was it?'

He smiled at her ruefully. 'A place where I feel at home, someone to feel at home with. I suppose you might say, to be loved for myself. Trite, but true.' He looked down into his glass as he continued, his smile withering on the crooked vine of his mouth.

'Of course, if you consider that the self that you are is more worthy of hatred and contempt than of love, it's very difficult to persuade yourself that it's even worth trying to change for the better. I'm not a religious man but deep down I do believe that you reap what you sow, particularly where human relationships are concerned. I also believe that pride goes before a fall, and mine was monumental in both cases.'

The bitter note of ironic self-mockery in his voice pierced her compassionate heart to the quick and she knew suddenly, with apalling certainty, what he was trying to tell her. *She* was the cause of his dramatic change of attitude and lifestyle over the past few years. By blindly striking out at him in her pain she had changed something fundamental in him, at once and forever. Her random act of emotional vandalism had caused him to build a whole new image of himself around a lie.

He saw the horrified knowledge dawn in her eyes and interpreted it as something else.

'You have every right to look disbelieving, Claudia, but I assure you that I'm a completely different man from the one I was two years ago. OK, sometime I lapse,' he corrected himself, his determination to be relentlessly honest painfully visible. 'I'm human—but in general I've conquered the personal demons that had me ride roughshod over other people's dreams. I know you probably thought that I callously shrugged off what happened that day, that I never even bothered to think about you again. But I did. I do. I stayed out of your life and kept Mark out too because I believed that was what you wanted, that that was the least painful alternative for you. But if you had ever been in trouble I would have known—would have helped you. But you didn't even grant me that small penance. You managed very well for yourself.'

'How—how would you have known I needed help?' Claudia asked shakily, her skin crawling with renewed guilt.

'I had a friend in Auckland check up on you occasionally. Nothing intrusive—just the bare bones,' he assured her quickly, seeing the sudden distaste in her eyes. 'To see that you weren't in any dire straits—whether you had a job and if you seemed happy.'

The knowledge that he had been watching over her all this time, however casually and intermittently, gave her strange chills. While he had been facing his demons, she had been hiding from hers. She was still hiding.

'Are you sure you don't want some more wine?' he asked, and she realised that she had raised her empty glass to her lips to conceal their trembling.

'Oh, no—no, thank you. Er—perhaps some coffee.' She had used the computer earlier and with Morgan's help chosen an up-and-coming New Zealand-born driver for the hotel to sponsor. Now what she needed was something to counter the volatile compound of guilt and alcohol that mingled in her veins.

Morgan collected their empty plates and excused himself to carry them back into the terracotta-tiled coolness of the interior of the house. Claudia narrowed her eyes against the sun slanting in over the glittering waters of the harbour, and tried to let the sheer beauty of the view calm her unquiet spirit.

Morgan's whitewashed concrete house, a tribute to modern engineering, seemed to grow out from the very side of the cliff, the high-sided balcony on which they sat curving out over a breathtakingly sheer drop to the winding tarmac of Marine Drive below.

Leaning on the rough-cast top of the balcony, Claudia tilted her head to let the warm sunlight wash over her face and bare arms. She had put on a soft cardigan-jacket when she had set out in the overcast morning but was glad now that she had worn a yellow dress with tiny, loose cap-sleeves underneath. The smoothly under-turned ends of her blow-dried hair flirted in and out of the little stand-up collar as a breeze that was a far cry from Wellington's reputedly fierce windiness drifted gently in off the sea.

From here she had a perfect view of the irregular sweep of small bays that scalloped the eastern shores of the harbour. Way down to the left she could see the narrow wooden tongue of the wharf at Eastbourne poking cheekily out into the sea, a ferry wallowing squatly at its side. And across in the western haze lay the compact building blocks of the central city, crouched beneath the hills that rose sharply behind it, creating the steep inner-city suburbs that had astonished Claudia when she had first had cause to visit one or two apparently vertical streets and note the property-owners' hair-raising answers to providing accessible driveways. She smiled at the memory.

'You see—a little sloth is good for us all. You look very contented out here in the sun.' Morgan's return with the coffee-tray took her off-guard, but there was no trace of his sombre mood of a few minutes ago as he relaxed opposite and began to pour the coffee. In black polo-shirt and white designer jeans he looked very Continental. 'Aren't you glad you came? We get on well together, don't we? There's hardly been a single cross word between us in the past two weeks.'

'But that's because——' Claudia stopped and he lounged more comfortably in his chair.

'Because?' he invited lazily, his blue eyes almost the same colour as the shifting, sun-lit sea behind him.

'Because you've been putting yourself out to be...co-operative,' she said grudgingly.

'Co-operative?' His quizzical smile flicked at her hesitant choice of words.

'Pleasant,' she clarified with even greater reluctance, concious that that twinkle in his eye was a great deal more attractive than it should be.

'Only pleasant? I must be slipping,' he murmured. 'I thought I was being thoroughly charming.'

'I've had a lot of practice at seeing through charming fakes,' said Claudia, almost burning her tongue on her coffee before she remembered she usually took milk.

'Do you mean when you were with Nash? I guess that in any situation like his there are an inevitable number of hangers-on, hoping some of the glamour will rub off...'

At least he was no longer classing *her* as one of the groupies!

'Chris liked to have lots of people around him. He loved the crowds and the parties.'

'But you didn't,' he guessed shrewdly.

'I didn't say that,' she said, her sensitivity quick to sense criticism where there was none. 'I was young and in love with a famous man. I liked to have fun, to meet new people. We could go anywhere in the world and be swamped with invitations——'

'Was that what you fell in love with—the glory rather than the substance of the man?'

'Actually when I fell in love with him I didn't know he was famous,' she said tartly. 'He was recuperating from an accident and hiding out from the Press. He came to stay at the country inn my parents owned. He was there for three weeks.'

'And when he left?'

She lifted her sharp chin in a mixture of bravado and defiance. 'I left with him.'

And in spite of subsequent events she had never regretted it. If she had stayed within the narrow, blinkered world that her parents inhabited she would never have discovered the true richness of living. Looking back, her childhood had been amazingly arid. It seemed that she had spent all her youth desperately seeking the approval of parents who believed that to praise was to encourage sinful vanity. They had rigidly adhered to the principle that sparing the rod spoiled the child and, as an only child, Claudia had been constantly monitored and pressured to conform to their traditional concept of female modesty and subservience. Dutiful obedience was the only proof of love that they recognised or required and Claudia was taught.

Chris had burst like a dazzling revelation into that joyless existance, embodying all the secret yearnings of her imprisoned young heart. For him love had been easy—bright with laughter, warmth and golden pleasure and wonderfully liberating to Claudia's strait-jacketed emotions.

'You still didn't realise who he was?'

'Of course I did. He didn't mislead me, if that's what you're implying,' Claudia said. 'He told me who he was, what he did for a living, what it would be like——'

'It must have sounded exciting. But still, the reality must have been a bit of a shock—especially for an over-protected country girl.'

It annoyed her that he so swiftly analysed her home life, laying its deficiencies bare in just a few well-chosen words. 'I adjusted,' she said stubbornly. 'It wasn't just a fling, you know, to relieve the boredom of his convalescence. He didn't have to ask me to go with him. He loved me.'

'You're very loyal, aren't you, Claudia?' he murmured, the steam from his cup momentarily obscuring the expression in his eyes. 'Was he really such a shining paragon of manhood? Is that the kind of woman you are, one who needs to hero-worship her man?'

'No, of course not,' Claudia responded hotly, 'but you seem to be trying to imply that Chris somehow took unfair advantage of me. I *wanted* to go with him. I was twenty years old and I might have been innocent and over-protected in some ways, but intellectually I was probably more mature than most girls my age. I knew what I was doing—that there would be no going back.

'In fact, in some ways I felt older than Chris,' she admitted revealingly. 'He'd always lived such a charmed life. He never really knew what it was like to lose at anything. And he was always so... optimistic about life, so open about his feelings... so—boyishly trusting that everything would turn out all right in the end... as if life were just a great game to be enjoyed. He had to be like that, I suppose, or he'd never have survived the incredible stresses of motor racing, but it could be quite irritating sometimes, when I wanted him to take something seriously and he'd just grin and tell me not to worry, that everything would be OK.'

'Do you ever wonder whether you might have been outgrowing him by the time he died?' said Morgan quietly.

'No, of *course* not! I was going to marry him!' she blurted out heedlessly, the fervency of her denial repressing the doubts that still lingered inside her.

'There was never any mention of marriage in the papers.'

She couldn't tell from his expression whether he believed her or not and all of a sudden it was important he did.

'It was a secret... Chris had arranged for us to go to Las Vegas the day after his race. No one knew about it. We were going to announce it afterwards. He liked doing that—putting one over on the Press, springing surprises on his friends. But instead of a marriage that week there was a funeral...'

She had felt guilty about that, too; the feeling that his death had somehow opened a cage door. Previously, she had fended off Chris's confidently light-hearted proposals, uneasy with the knowledge that they seemed to be spending less and less time together as his driving successes mounted. With his usual quick-fire optimism Chris had decided that her problem was a lack of security that their marriage would solve but Claudia had been less certain. Two or three years before she would have jumped at his offer but with more worldly experience under her belt she had been quietly beginning to question whether the love that she bore him was strong enough to survive a lifetime of public scrutiny and private stress over his risk-laden choice of career, one that she knew he would never voluntarily give up.

Her pregnancy had pre-empted her vague thoughts of leaving and she had allowed Chris's genuine joy at the prospect of their child to overwhelm her misgivings. Whatever his other failings she knew that he would love his child with all the warmth of his volatile nature. He might be a bit irresponsible as a day-to-day parent but no child of his would ever have cause to feel like a burden or a duty. Claudia had felt that she owed it to their baby to give it the early security of a real family, to at least give the marriage a fighting chance...

'No wonder you felt the need to escape the media circus that followed. You must have been feeling very vulnerable...'

A muscle jumped in Morgan's cheek and she realised wretchedly that he was probably reinterpreting her seemingly promiscuous plunge into another man's arms so soon after her lover's death in an entirely new and erroneously compassionate light.

Tell him.

'Morgan, I——'

'Did you ever think of perhaps going back to your parents?' he cut across her faltering beginning.

She unknowingly flinched at the suggestion. 'My parents were very... insular people, very strict in their principles. Decent people don't show affection or touch each other in front of others, you see—even if they're married or members of the same family. In fact they

were so humiliated by my notorious fall from grace that
they couldn't hold up their heads in the community
they'd lived all their lives in. They sold the hotel not
long after I left and moved to Australia. I haven't spoken
to them in years.'

'What parents put their children through in the name
of pride,' Morgan murmured and she knew that he was
thinking of his own experiences—first as a son and then
from the diametrically opposed perspective of be-
leaguered fatherhood. From what he had let drop about
his business she knew that he had never fully reconciled
with his own parents after his enforced teenage marriage. What he had achieved he had done so without the
inheritance that his youthful pride had rejected as a bribe.
When his parents had died their entire estate had been
put in trust for Mark.

'And yet you encouraged Mark to open the lines of
communication with *me* . . . so you must believe in the
importance of family relationships . . .' he said softly.

'I didn't think you believed me about that,' Claudia
remembered grimly.

He bluntly conceded her point. 'I didn't—at the time.
Mark told me later that it was your chipping away at
his stubbornness that wore him down into agreeing to
see me.'

His voice was low with impatience. He was far less
interested in the known facts of his own past than in the
mysteries of hers. Her reactions to him were so erratic—
tacitly inviting and yet overtly rejecting—that he knew
there must be some powerful psychological inhibitor in
operation.

Claudia seemed to have a subconscious fascination
with the forbidden, perhaps as a result of those for-
mative years in which an impulsive child had been drilled
to maintain a prematurely adult self-control. But she was
also intelligent and self-aware. The prospect of being out

of control, sexually or emotionally, was probably as threatening as it was irresistibly exciting.

At least he *hoped* it was going to prove irresistible!

The great temptation was to use her potent sexual awareness of him to bludgeon rather than seduce, to force her to the point where she would either admit to her fears or succumb to him in spite of then, thus neutralising their threat.

As temptations went the idea held a savage allure. It also had the potential to backfire to devastating effect.

'Have you tried to contact your parents recently?'

'Since I became respectable, you mean?' Claudia murmured cynically, wondering what on earth was going on behind that cloudless blue gaze to cause him to look broodingly male, as sultry as a summer storm about to break out of a clear sky. Even his question had been uttered in a husky growl, like the distant rumble of warning thunder, she thought nervously.

'I'll never be that as far as they're concerned. I...I wrote to them about—when I knew I was pregnant.' She immediately hated herself for the feeble prevarication. 'They sent my opened letter back in a plain envelope. That's all—no note, no message. A fairly explicit rejection, I thought.' Her twisted smile belied the uncaring shrug. 'I suppose an illegitimate baby was no less than they expected of me. Maybe they were afraid that if they gave me the slightest sign of encouragement I might turn up on their doorstep one day with my tainted child in tow...' She tailed off. Even though her childhood had been less than idyllic, it hurt to think that to her parents she no longer existed.

'It was their loss, Claudia. You baby would have been a beautiful child. As you would have been a fine mother.'

The simple comments tore at her heart. Tears stung her eyes and she tried to pretend it was the sun. She looked down at the fingers clenched in her lap and didn't see him stand up and come around the table. Not until he crouched by her chair, his hands sliding warmly over her cold ones, did she realise what she had done. She had invited him this close with her appalling weakness!

'You don't know that——' She tried to pull her hands away but he wouldn't let her. 'It was all a horrible mistake, anyway. You were right when you said that it was a blessing that I lost him——'

'I never said that,' he denied quietly, his thumbs moving gently over her tense white knuckles. 'And you didn't *lose* your son. That implies carelessness and I know you're not that——'

'It was sheer carelessness to get pregnant in the first place,' she said, the tears finally spilling over as she stiffly rejected his comfort, still refusing to look at his face, upturned to hers. Not for two years, she thought with a wrench, had she been so recklessly emotional as to cry in front of someone else. That time it had been him, too...

'Was it? Who was taking care of contraception—him or you?'

Now Claudia was flushed among her tears. He thought he was asking about his son—whether it was *Mark* who had been irresponsible. Hadn't she caused him torment enough?

'Me. And I didn't forget. Not once. It was just one of those things.' The irony of her phrasing hit her as she realised that those were the very words that the doctor had used to console her after her baby's death.

'I didn't want to get pregnant, I didn't even want a baby,' she said starkly. There! Perhaps that would be enough to put him off, stop him tormenting her with his compassion...

'Then it certainly wasn't carelessness. It was a miracle. The miracle of conception. You might not have wanted a baby, Claudia, but you wanted *your* baby, didn't you...?'

She thought the moistness on the back of her hands was the tears that had escaped her vigilance, but it was his mouth. She stared at his dark head, bent over her lap, and watched, shocked, as he drew her hands aside and kissed the gentle curve of her stomach just below the slim white belt that separated the narrow yellow skirt from the buttoned bodice of her dress.

'Don't——'

She could feel the heat of his mouth smouldering through the thin fabric and her hands clenched protestingly around his. He raised his head and moved their entwined fingers to stroke where he had kissed.

'You were wretchedly ill all through your pregnancy—Mark did tell me that much—and you had a terrifying experience of childbirth. Did the doctor tell you that you might have similar problems with future pregnancies? Was there any permanent damage?'

'I—no. He—he said that... that my health had been stressed even before I got pregnant—that otherwise I was—was quite normal... and that I shouldn't have any trouble conceiving again if I wanted to...' She couldn't concentrate on her words, not when he was looking at her with that peculiar gravity, his knuckles brushing gently back and forth over her dress, his lids sinking sensuously down over his eyes as she stumbled over the word that suddenly seemed indecently tangled on her tongue.

'And do you want to? Or are you frightened by the bad memories... afraid to risk ever getting pregnant again?'

Why had he said *risk* in that slightly disparaging way, as if he expected her to cringe at the prospect? Did he think she was that neurotic? She hesitated, sensing some kind of trap, but not being able to distinguish where it lay.

'Would you like another baby, Claudia?' he persisted softly, almost tauntingly. His hand stopped guiding hers in its provocative stroking, pressing instead into the taut resilience of her belly, the masculine-enwrapped femininity fisted over her womb. 'Another son or daughter.'

'I——' She licked her dry lips and whispered helplessly, 'Some day, I suppose. I'm not...I mean, I don't—it wouldn't be the same——'

'Of course it wouldn't,' he agreed quietly. 'This time you would plan carefully for your pregnancy. Make sure that you were properly healthy before you conceived, prepared both mentally and physically, financially and emotionally secure.'

'I—yes—I suppose, yes, I would——' She felt as if she was being lured along a secret path, whose intriguing twists and turns obscured its destination. The hot sun poured down on her head. Morgan, on his knees facing her, was in the shadow cast by her figure, and the expression in his eyes... She went very still.

'It wouldn't be a replacement, but, if you had another baby whose father was from the same genetic background as the father of your son, the child would probably grow up to share many of the physical characteristics that your son would have had...'

She was suffering from heat-stroke. He couldn't *possibly* be suggesting what she thought he was suggesting in that deep, slow, calm voice! Her lashes spiky with tears, her eyes golden with shock, she listened to him utter the shattering proposition, 'I told you I owed you a debt, Claudia, and that it couldn't be paid in words. As I see it, the only way for me to truly heal the breach between us and redeem my honour is to repay exactly what I deprived you of: a life for a life.

'I can't bring your son back, but I could give you another. Only this time I wouldn't be grandfather but father to your child. And, if you're as honest as I'm trying to be, I think you'll admit that the act of making our baby would be an immensely pleasurable and deeply sensual experience for both of us...'

CHAPTER EIGHT

CLAUDIA opened her eyes.

'W-what happened?'

'I'm not sure, but it looked to me like a good old-fashioned swoon.'

Claudia struggled to sit up among the sinkingly soft cushions of the brick-coloured sofa, only vaguely recognising the white room with the terracotta floor and Turkish rugs as being somewhere in the cool depths of Morgan's clifftop house. Surely it had all been a dream; an impossible, improbable dream... She pushed a shaky hand through her hair and looked at the man sitting patiently beside her, his hip level with hers.

'I—how did I get here?' she murmured with confusion. She didn't remember any of the warning dizziness that usually presaged a faint.

'I carried you.' He held a chilled glass to her lips.

Water. She sipped it gratefully, moistening her dry lips. She tucked her hair behind her ears and lowered her hand to her throat, where she discovered her collar and several buttons undone and a necklace of tiny wet droplets across her exposed collarbone. Her belt had also been removed, she noticed. She leaned back against the cushions that were piled behind her shoulders, nervously fingering an empty buttonhole.

'Was I out for long?'

'Not long enough for me to ravish you,' he said drily, his perception as acute as ever as he replaced the glass on a squat wooden table beside the couch. 'That bodice is quite tight and I thought it was a good idea to ease the constriction over your chest and cool you down with a few splashes of water.'

There was no anger in his expression but there was no gleam of mocking amusement, either, and she was shocked to realise how much she missed it. She deserved the set-down. She had insulted both his honour and his manhood with her momentary suspicion that he might have taken advantage of her helplessness.

'Thank you,' she murmured awkwardly, not knowing quite how to apologise. She wanted to do up her dress again, but her wicked imagination now turned even the modest act of doing up the buttons into a subtly pro-vocative performance that would draw attention to her womanly curves. Instead she merely dabbed at the dampness on her throat with her unsteady fingers.

'My pleasure.' He reached into his jeans and produced a clean, pressed handkerchief. 'Allow me.'

His eyes were lowered, his lashes concealing his expression as he gently mopped away the beading of water that she had smeared into a wet slick across her upper chest. His touch was gentle, the blunt features and square jaw tight with absorption as he concentrated on his simple task.

He was very thorough, Claudia thought breathlessly as the moments ticked endlessly by. He had to part the edges of her dress a little more to catch the drops that had succumbed to the force of gravity, holding first one side and then the other out of the way as his hand slipped under the gaping fabric and patted the soft cotton over her bare skin.

It seemed to take him a long time to dry her to his complete satisfaction but Claudia didn't protest, staring resolutely at the hollow at the base of his throat, aware of the hush around them, the soft rasp of their breathing.

His hand finally stilled against her, the handkerchief tucked into the exposed hollow between her breasts where the tiny white bow that concealed the front catch of her bra just peeked above the first fastened button. She felt a tiny tug and that button, too, fell open. Her eyes flew to his face.

He was waiting for her, his smile blazing with sensuous challenge as he flicked open another button, and another.

'*Now* you can plead ravishment...'

He plunged his hands around her waist under the thin fabric, raking the bodice wide open. But instead of bending over her submissive figure he lifted her sharply up against him, his fingers tightly constricting around the base of her ribcage as he positioned her mouth under his.

Her gasp was absorbed by the swift, rough thrust of his tongue and a low growl greeted her instinctive impulse to ease the pressure around her waist by gripping his shoulders. Once there, gravity was again a powerfully seductive force as her hands slid helplessly down over the straining muscles of his back, her fingers digging in for purchase as she used his steely strength to arch herself against him.

'*Yes*...' The hiss of triumphant satisfaction sizzled in the dark cavern of her mouth as he devoured her ungoverned response, twisting so that he pulled her half across his knees. One hand unwrapped itself from her waist to splay across her breasts, his thumb and fingertip stretching possessively from peak to lacy peak. Held tightly against his hardness and consumed by his softness, Claudia gloried in the erotic contrasts of his maleness, the brutal strength that was tempered by the heat of passion, the thickening need that bespoke his ability both to lose control and to wield it to exquisite effect.

When his mouth broke away from hers her head fell back with a shuddering sigh.

'I take it this means you've decided that you like being ravished,' he said thickly.

She lifted her head. She had made no conscious decisions, she had just flowed with the desires of the moment. 'I——'

The hand on her breast pressed lightly against their weight. 'All you need to answer is yes.'

'W-what was the question?' A breath of caution rippled across her dreamy pool of sensual delight.

'You know what it was...'

'I—you weren't serious!' Her whispered protest was without conviction. The grave intensity in his stunning blue eyes was terrifying.

'Wasn't I?' he asked steadily, his hand moving to settle firmly over her left breast, and the hot, uneven thump of her heart. 'Then why did you swoon?'

Swoon. It sounded so weak and ineffectual, so Victorian for the modern career woman she strove to be.

'I fainted, that's all,' she said more firmly. 'The wine and the sun——'

'And the shock. You shock easily, don't you, Claudia, for all your worldly experience ...?' He studied her pale mouth, and the flush on her cheeks, her wide brown eyes shadowed with deep secrets. He bent over her to murmur, 'Is the idea of having my baby really so shocking?'

Utterly. It was indecent. Wicked of her even to contemplate it. Wicked of him to make her want it. His mouth was a kiss away from hers. She turned her head aside, her throat arching in resistance to his enticing invitation.

'Any woman would be shocked to be, to be——'

'Desired?'

'What you're talking about isn't desire——' she began raggedly.

'True. *This* is desire.' His other arm tightened around her waist, pressing her firmly down in his lap as he shifted his thighs, the small undulation of his hips imprinting the firm outline of his masculinity against her soft bottom.

'So don't think that I'm offering to make love to you out of mere altruism,' he warned softly, his breath warm and sweet in her burning ear. 'I want you, Claudia—badly enough to try to stack the deck in my favour with every incentive I can think of. I know you want me, too——' his thumb scraped gently across the stiffened peak of her breast to prove his point '—but you think the wrongs of the past too important to ignore. This way you don't have to feel guilty about betraying your past by taking me for your lover. You can have it all: me *and* your revenge——'

'You don't have to do this,' she said desperately. 'I don't want revenge. It wasn't your *fault*! You...you can't want a baby with me——'

'Why can't I?' Her much agonised confession was ruthlessly shouldered aside as Morgan stubbornly pursued his own ends. 'Is it only women who are allowed to yearn for children? Last time around I was working so hard that I missed out on most of Mark's childhood. I was so busy proving what a successful businessman I was that I was virtually an absentee parent. I didn't put enough effort into being the kind of ordinary, everyday father a child can relate to. I know that I'll be a far better father this time...'

His confident use of the present tense edged her on to the verge of panic. But the word 'yearn' made Claudia's tender heart stagger.

'But—Mark——'

'Ah, yes, Mark.' His mouth firmed into a grim line. 'The magic banner you brandish whenever you want to fend me off. Let's talk about Mark. Are you worried I'm exhibiting some obscure form of sexual deviance by lusting after my son's former mistress?'

His words were crudely effective but Claudia refused to flinch. 'Are you?'

A glint of grim humour smouldered in the dazzling blue. 'Lusting after you? Certainly. But you and I know there's a great deal more than that between us. A man doesn't offer a baby to every object of his desire. Perhaps it's not my motives so much as my potency you're afraid to trust?'

'I can hardly doubt that, can I?'

Again that wicked undulation of his hips which sent heat coursing through her veins and flattering her skin. 'True.'

'I *meant* considering that you had Mark.' She tried to quell him with a haughty look, confused by the teasing that had come hard on the heels of his ardent seriousness.

'That was a long time ago, but I have no reason to think that the years of abstinence have diminished my fertility,' he responded with suspicious gravity.

'Abstinence!' The glowing gold flecks in Claudia's eyes expressed her fierce scorn of that idea.

'I meant from having children,' he said meekly. 'I've always used condoms when I slept with other women, Claudia. I wasn't going to risk another accidental pregnancy.' His thick, dark lashes suddenly veiled the searing blue gaze as it sank to the rapid rise and fall of her semi-exposed breasts. 'I'm looking forward to the novelty of being naked inside you. I'm curious as to how it will feel. I'm sure it will be a very intense experience for both of us. Are you, or have you recently been, on the Pill?'

Still stunned by the graphic description of his sexual eagerness, she responded with automatic truthfulness. 'No, but——'

'Good. Then there's no inhibition to your own fertility. Does that mean that it's been a fairly long time for you, too, Claudia?'

'A long time?' she repeated his gentle enquiry blankly.

'Since you allowed a man to——' His words were dammed by her flying fingers as her hand shot up to prevent him uttering the rest of the shatteringly indecent comment. He kissed her smothering palm, his sinful tongue darting out to trace the sensitive creases as his eyes mocked her over his fleshly gag.

She hurriedly withdrew her tingling hand but he still held her flustered gaze captive with his triumphant one.

'You can stop me saying it but we're both thinking about it, aren't we? It's very erotic, the thought of you and me nude together, without any artificial barriers between us, creating something beautiful out of our joining, something sweet and precious...'

Claudia could feel her body melting into the masculine strength that surrounded her, enchanted by the spell of his sensual poetry. Perhaps, if his need and desire were so great, she could make private peace with her unquiet conscience by giving him what he wanted, and in the process steal a little happiness from under the very nose of wretched fate...

'Actually, I find the thought of your pregnancy extremely erotic, too,' he murmured, lowering his head to kiss the warm swell of her breast above her bra. 'I like the idea of making love to you while my baby ripens inside you, of exploring your new sensitivities, of watching your body change and grow as it prepares to welcome a new life into the world...a new beginning...'

She stiffened, as she realised what he was suggesting. 'You mean, you'd expect...? But, I thought...'

'Very soon you're going to run out of those all-purpose buts, and then where will you be?' Morgan commented drily. 'I suppose that, as usual, you assume the very worst of me. What did you think I meant? A one-night stand of guaranteed hot-and-fertile sex at the receptive peak of your hormonal cycle? A brief affair to be broken off the instant that conception is confirmed?'

Claudia flushed miserably and squirmed, but he would not let her escape either his grasp or his censure.

'Damn you, Duchess, if I had intended to be merely a sperm donor I would have suggested artificial insemination,' he said roughly. 'I'm not going to get you pregnant and then cut and run like some irresponsible kid! Naturally I'll look after you during your pregnancy...given your medical history you'll need the extra security of my support and involvement. And, well...' the smooth descent from crisp command into slow drawl alerted her to the probability of fresh outrage '...it's an accepted fact that many pregnant women experience a sudden increase in their sex drive. In the best interests of your general health and well-being I would make sure that *all* your cravings were satisfied...'

She felt waves of heat wash over her. 'How—how very self-sacrificing of you,' she managed, in a trembling voice that failed miserably to be sarcastic.

'Isn't it?' he purred, his hands beginning to move against her again in a very disturbing way. 'How can you possibly deny a man on such a noble quest?'

Oh, God. Claudia knew that the only way to fight the fierce desire flooding through her mind and body was to have him battling on her side. She closed her eyes, and said a silent goodbye to the glorious, sensual gloating of his touch.

'Morgan...?'

'Don't worry, Duchess. Don't worry about anything. Let me take care of you and our baby...I promise to make it good for you...'

'The baby——'

'Will be as perfect as we can make it. And if that's not absolutely perfect, well, we'll love her anyway, as the most innocent part of ourselves...'

Oh, God. Why did he have to be so damned *fine*! Tears welled up behind her closed eyes as she contemplated what she was about to lose. 'No! No, I mean the *other* baby. *My* baby. My son.' She was very careful to stress the exclusivity of her possession. 'I saw him...afterwards...I asked and they showed him to me——'

She felt him still, sensed the new physical tension that entered his limbs. 'Oh?'

It was a very careful, very neutral response, thought Claudia bitterly as she opened her eyes. His hard features were quiet, composed, and very, very wary. He did well to fear the trend of the conversation.

'He had dark hair and...and—I don't know what colour his eyes were...I never saw them open.' That had troubled her, haunted her for a long time. She stumbled on, 'There was a funeral service——'

The tension in the arms holding her tightened, his eyes still locked with hers. 'And you were alone—I'm sorry——'

'And a christening,' she cut him off quickly, before he could undermine her courage with his sympathy. 'I had him christened first—so that he could be buried with a name, not just as a...a thing...but as a person, who belonged to somebody.'

'Claudia——'

She shook her head. 'Do you want to know what I called him?' she went on relentlessly.

Some of the tension drained out of him. 'If you want to tell me.'

He thought it was going to be as simple as a name. She almost hated him at that moment for his unwitting ignorance.

'Christopher!' she said fiercely. 'I called him Chris!'

'A fine name for a boy,' he said calmly, and she couldn't believe that an intelligent man could be so wilfully stupid.

'Chris! After his *father*.' She could no longer hold his steady gaze. She looked down at her hands pushing against his rock-solid chest, trying to prise her out of the hideously inappropriate intimacy of his embrace. 'Christopher Nash Lawson!'

There was no immediate response and Claudia couldn't help darting a look at his face, as unreadably still as the rest of him. Why, oh, why wasn't he letting her go, shoving her away in disgust?

'Mark and I weren't even lovers!' she cried angrily, fisting her hands as she struggled futilely against his implacable calmness. 'Dammit, don't you *understand*?'

'I understand perfectly. You're telling me that Mark wasn't the father of your baby.'

Now it was her turn to still. Something in the way he said it, the easy self-control that was in marked contrast to the blast of hot-tempered condemnation she had expected, the sheer lack of hostility when he had every right to feel bitterly betrayed...

'You *knew*!' Her fists fell weakly into her lap as the instinctive certainty overwhelmed her. 'All along, you *knew*...!'

'Not all along,' he confirmed bluntly. 'Not until several months afterwards, in fact. I went back to see you—or at least I revisited your home and found out that you'd moved. Your neighbour was very informative, though, very sorry for all that you had gone through...losing your baby so late...at *seven* months.'

Only now, when it was too late for her to remove herself to a safe distance, did he relinquish his binding grip, instead massaging his flattened palms up and down her arms, as if he could feel the inner chill that sapped her will and the energy to move her limbs.

'You knew...' It was still sinking in, her thoughts a frozen mass of confusion as the implications of his confession gradually began to percolate into her mind. He knew that his son wasn't the father of the child she lost. But...that didn't make sense!

'How...how much do you know?'

'Everything.'

It was hard to take. 'You *couldn't* have known . . . all the things you've said——' Her voice was as broken as her thoughts. 'And just now, before I fainted—what you said about the father's genes——'

'I knew that if I gave you enough openings you were eventually bound to trust me with the truth,' he said simply.

'You mean—you said all those things *deliberately*?' she demanded wildly, trying to remember everything that she had ever said to him. And all the time that she had been evading the consequences of her actions, had been fending him off with lies and half-truths, he had *known*!

Shame engulfed her, then defensive anger. 'You were trying to trap me!' she accused rawly.

'How can the truth be a trap, Claudia?' he murmured, his hands still generating the warmth of friction against her clammy skin. 'You know that you wanted to tell me . . . I didn't force it out of you.'

The knowledge that he was right didn't resolve the violent conflict inside her. All that mental torment—for *nothing*!

'You could have told me!' she choked.

'It was your story to tell, Duchess, not mine.' His sombre smile was like salt in the wound.

'And what if I had never told you?' she challenged.

'Well, then, I would have respected your silence.'

To her horror she believed him. 'And all that about having your baby?' she asked hoarsely. 'That was just a way to . . . to make me tell you . . . ?'

'I don't make promises I don't intend to keep.' Morgan picked up one nerveless hand from her lap and held it briefly against his mouth before drawing it to his chest. She suddenly realised that her bodice was still gaping and her other hand came up to clutch it closed. 'As far as I'm concerned nothing is different. *I* haven't changed my mind. Have you?'

'You must hate me...' she whispered. She knew that *she* would, if their situations were reversed.

'I had hurt you and you retaliated in the only way available to you at the time,' he told her, with a gentle understanding that lanced old wounds. 'Of course I was angry—I was gut-wrenchingly furious at first, which was one of the reasons why I decided to keep track of you, but I've had two years to come to terms with it and, since I met you again, I've realised that that impulsive lie was probably as painful for you as it was for me. After all, whatever the baby's parentage, I *did* cause you to fall and lose him...'

Her lips formed a hushed O of dismay as the significance of the last sentence hit her squarely in the chest, congesting it with thickening horror as he continued, 'You don't find it easy to inflict pain on others, do you, Duchess, even when you think it's justified? Why don't you let me show you how much easier it's going to be for you to inflict pleasure...?'

And he showed her, by leaning forward and covering her parted mouth with his own, feeding her with the strength of his desire.

Under his kiss she acknowledged that her courage had already exceeded its limits. She couldn't bear the thought of now confessing an even greater betrayal of her honour. She desperately wanted to accept his assurance that he knew everything, even though it was now achingly obvious that he didn't.

Her wonderful reprieve was only temporary, but suddenly she no longer cared. Let the future take care of itself. She wasn't going to risk having to wait another two years before his anger abated enough for Morgan to accept her in his arms again, if he ever could. She needed him *now*, right this moment. She needed the passion that could heal her, the desire that she could use to express her silent remorse, her unspoken love...

He slid her off his lap, turning into her as she half lay, half sat on the couch beside him. The hand that had been guarding her disarray reached for him, burrowing under his shirt until he impatiently pulled it over his head, ruffling the dark hair on his head and leaving her awed at the first sight of his bareness. He was broad and strong, a light tan sculpting the rippling muscles which were exposed by his smooth, almost hairless chest. She touched him, tentatively, on the hard ridge of bone centred between the flat, male nipples.

'Disappointed?'

Her startled eyes flew to his steamy gaze. 'Some women equate masculinity with a hairy chest. I assure you, I'm not less of a man for my lack.'

It stunned her that he could believe that he needed to reassure her of the fact.

'I know.' Her hand flattened and he let out a hiss of breath, the ridging of his flat belly above the leather-belted trousers clenching in a ripple that vibrated up under his skin to tease her fingertips.

'Now it's my turn.' He peeled back the edges of her dress, this time pushing it off her shoulders and gently pulling her arms free of the sleeves.

She watched his face, the sultry fascination that drew his features tight as he reached for the decorative bow between the lacy cups of her bra and smoothly curved his fingers around the plastic clip.

'You've done this before,' she said, unable to help the breathy expression of her nervousness. She had always needed two hands to undo the secure catch but he was revealing a single-handed skill.

'But never with such delicious anticipation,' he said with a glibness that might have offended her if she hadn't been watching the smouldering intentness of his gaze, the quivering flare of his nostrils as he scented the faint natural perfume of her body and drew it inside himself. The tiny snick of the catch sounded thunderingly loud to her ears and she closed her eyes, the better to concentrate on the joy of his first caress.

Nothing happened and, aching for his touch but too shy to articulate her need, she lifted heavy lids to find him studying her face with savage masculine pleasure. Satisfied that he had her fullest attention, he very slowly eased away the intricate lace, taking care not to touch her, never taking his eyes off hers. Only when the fragile straps had slid down her arms did he lower his eyes again. For a breathless moment there was utter silence.

'I can see your heart beating,' he said huskily, still not touching her, and she looked down at herself and saw that it was true: the rigid peak of her left breast was visibly pulsing in time with the quickened internal rhythm inside her chest. The creamy flesh around it seemed to quiver with each tiny rise and fall, a delicate but explicit invitation that made her blush to see it. It seemed so terribly brazen, a bold flaunting of her physical desire for him, that her blush spread inexorably down over every inch of exposed skin, tautening her breasts even further with the warm, tingling excitement of sensual awareness.

Morgan smiled, intent on his prize, and his voice was thick with velvety promise as he cupped his hand around the flushed offering. 'So when I taste you I shall literally have your heart in my mouth.' He bent his head, so slowly that Claudia bit her lip to stop herself crying out in frustration.

At last she felt the hot, silky moistness surrounding and absorbing her aching flesh as he suckled her with exquisite finesse, and this time she did cry out, only to suffer the agony of having him lift his head.

'Am I hurting you?'

Her hand sank into his crisp, short hair, tugging him back. 'No...yes...please—don't stop...'

His smile smouldered across her senses, his eyes burning in their vivid intensity. 'I'm yours to command,

Duchess.' The hand lifting her breast tightened possess-ively. 'All you have to do is tell me what you want and I'll do it for you. Your pleasure is my fitting reward...'

His dark head bent over her again and she arched into the sweet-savage pull of his clever mouth, knowing that she didn't have to tell him what she wanted, he knew— he would always know, seemed to sense her desires even before she did...

His lavish praise of her breasts went on and on until she was drenched in the promised pleasure and needing more, much more; she ran her hands across the broad striation of muscle on his curved back, her fingernails digging into the compact flesh in a piercingly articulate demand that brought a gloriously swift response.

With a few quick, economical twists and turns, Morgan stripped the rumpled sundress off her hips and disposed of his jeans with an expressive groan as, in his haste, the heavy fabric scraped across his heated arousal. He took longer to remove the white cotton panties she wore, seemingly fascinated by the demure contrast to her sexy bra, and enjoying the involuntary movements of her hips as he languidly caressed her last covering down her trembling thighs. She almost died of shocked delight when he brushed a deft kiss across the soft tri-angle of curls so dark against the pearly sheen of her inner thighs but the brief intimacy was withdrawn im-mediately as he shed his own modest white briefs.

His lack of haste allowed Claudia to study covertly the full power and beauty of his virility and when she realised that he had caught her sidelong glances of flat-teringly wide-eyed appraisal she instinctively attempted to protect her own body from his frank gaze. The dif-ferences between male and female apart, his physique was nearly perfect whereas Claudia's body had borne a child and she was suddenly aware of imperfections that had not mattered a few moments ago, in the throes of mindless abandonment.

He froze, one knee pressing down beside her supine body, the other foot still planted on the tiled floor.

'Am I pleasing to you, Claudia?' he murmured, making no attempt similarly to hide the blatancy of his desire. 'I hope so, because you're very, very appealing to me...especially like that, your lovely full breasts peeping at me through your fingers and the soft rounded thigh drawn up to shelter the hot dewy silk I'm aching to feel around me...' He shuddered lightly, throwing his head back as his whole body flexed with the acuteness of his need. He was proud of his passion, engendering a similar pride in Claudia as he looked down at her and asked bluntly, 'Can you ease that ache for me, Claudia? Will you touch me and taste me and pleasure me in the way that I need to be to feel completed?'

As he intended to complete her? Claudia's uncertainty vanished; his honesty, verging on the crude and yet also poetically erotic, was just what she needed to reassure her of her desirability. How could she refuse him anything that he asked of her? His passion, his tender consideration, his magnificent male vulnerability conquered all her inhibitions.

He must have read her answer in her eyes, in the graceful falling away of her protective limbs, for he was coming back to her, folding himself down over her restlessly shifting body, again with that slow, sensual appreciation that was both infuriating and inflaming, caging her eagerness with his incredible self-control until they were melted, skin to skin, full-length on the resilient softness of the cushioned couch. Even then he paused.

'Are you comfortable? Or would you rather move to the bedroom...?'

'I wish you'd stop asking so many questions,' Claudia murmured, a bubble of sheer joy making her voice ragged with laughter as she revelled in the intoxicating savour of his salty, satin-rough skin and the heady aroma of his masculine arousal.

'I can't help it.' His caressing amusement encouraged her mischievous delight in the the silken splendour he was unravelling for her dazzled senses. 'I'm a very articulate lover and making love with you has turned me into an unashamed sybarite. I want to indulge in all the sensual vices with you in such luxury and comfort that you'll want it to go on forever, and ever...'

He was as good as his word. Claudia knew that, whatever else she might be able to force herself to forget, the timeless beauty of his fiery passion would always be part of her. He praised, he urged, he groaned, he poured out the pleasure that he had promised her with an endless, inspiring energy that never faltered. He was violent and aggressive, tender and gentle, never content for her to be passively receptive but fiercely demanding of her totally wanton and greedily eager response.

His passionate prowess made a liar of him when, at one point, they tumbled heedlessly off the wide, luxurious couch and he scarcely missed a beat, taking her on the hard floor, the rough weave of a thin woven rug barely protecting her from the cool shock of hard terracotta as he cupped her bottom and roughly parted her legs to plunge tightly into her, a thick moan of sexual gratification wrenching from his throat as he drove himself, and Claudia, to new extremes of pleasure.

Afterwards he carried her remorsefully into his sunny bedroom and laid her on the soft white polished-cotton spread of his huge bed where he proceeded to render his apologies with an exquisite, unselfish delicacy. While she lay, still dazed with delicious exhaustion, he sat and placed his hand over her shivering belly and said boldly, 'I wonder if my baby is in here already, experiencing the first spark of joyous life?'

If Claudia hadn't already been flushed all over she would have blushed at his gloating eagerness. He was certainly taking no chances. He was making sure that his intentions were clearly understood and accepted.

'I doubt it, certainly not so soon,' she said repressively, pushing away her doubts.

'A few moments is all it takes,' he smiled, his fingers tracing around her sensitive navel.

'Conception isn't instantaneous, you know,' she said, trying to sound blasé. 'Anyway, it isn't really the best time for me right now—to conceive, I mean.'

His amazing eyes were deep blue with slumbrous satisfaction. 'I know you didn't mean to make love. It was very much the best time for that, wasn't it, Duchess? And now you've had the pleasure I hope you're not going to try and renege on the responsibility that you owe to me...' The finger rimming her navel slipped inside, making her stomach muscles flutter.

'Owe you?' Claudia could hardly concentrate on the words, her body attuned to his fingertip control.

'An old debt. All that money of mine that you frittered away two years ago. The money with which I bought off my obligation to my grandchild's mother...'

'Oh, that money,' murmured Claudia hazily. The soft pad of his finger withdrew and slipped inside again. 'I...I'll pay you back...' she offered, his silky taunt causing a nibble of guilt to eat at the fringes of her consciousness. She didn't know if he truly believed that she had used the money as frivolously as she had pretended but there was no denying she had allowed him to 'buy her off' under false pretences that still stood.

'Of course you will—in the most intimate and appropriate way imaginable.' His determined words were interspersed with soft kisses strung the length of her torso until Claudia felt the moist shock of his tongue replacing his finger in the small knotted recess in her belly. 'This baby will be our mutual gift of reparation. Accept it gratefully, as I am, in settlement of all outstanding debts between us....'

CHAPTER NINE

'SO WHAT practical plans have you made? What do you intend to do about your career when the baby's born? Juggle with a string of babysitters? Daycare? Or do you want me to pay for a live-in child-minder?'

Claudia gritted her teeth and shovelled the bacon and eggs that she had cooked on to Morgan's plate, striving for a lightness that she didn't feel.

'What is this, an interrogation?'

She turned back to the bench to pick up his coffee and pluck the toast from the toaster. She gave both pieces to Morgan and put in another slice for herself, not because she was hungry but because she needed an excuse to stay out of the hot seat across the table from that penetrating blue gaze.

She had no intention of letting him harass her into admitting that she didn't have any long-term plans. Such practicalities hadn't even entered her mind a week ago when she had succumbed to his persuasive seduction and now sheer terror at what the future might hold made her resolutely refuse to dwell on it. Her only thought then had been, if he could promise to love her baby, then perhaps was there a chance that he could also learn to love the baby's mother . . . ?

A foolish fantasy. He might care for her, but although guilt and desire were a potent mix they didn't add up to love. As frank as he was about everything else, if he loved her Morgan would have told her so. But a vital ingredient was missing from their relationship. Trust. On his side it was misplaced, and on hers deliberately withheld. As a lover he was exciting, passionate, tender, but she never let herself forget that he had been a brutally ambitious, impossibly demanding autocrat for many more years than he had been the compassionate and easygoing man he was emulating now. The cynical, ruthlessly manipulative side of him would never be entirely repressed; it was too ingrained, surfacing automatically whenever he felt thwarted ... or betrayed. He was quite capable of reverting, especially if he found out that his newly acquired persona had allowed him to be played for a fool.

Weighing up the risks, she had decided the pain of losing him was better postponed until she had hoarded up enough happiness to last her over the emotional winter that was sure to follow.

At least if she had his baby Claudia would always have a permanent link with him, an added dimension to her love that would give her life a richness of variety and purpose that had been lacking before. Morgan might deny her but he would never be able to bring himself to deny his child, whatever he felt about its mother. It was selfish, it was probably immoral but she was going to do it anyway. She was going to cheat fate.

'Just understandable interest. You are a cross-patch in the mornings, aren't you?' Morgan replied mildly as he attacked his breakfast. With his shirt unbuttoned and his chin unshaven he looked sensuously rumpled and regrettably sexy while Claudia, already carefully dressed in her hotel uniform, felt uncomfortably formal in her own kitchen.

'Is that why you haven't let me stay the night before now? Afraid I'd be disillusioned in the morning?'

No, afraid that he would become even more deeply embedded in her heart than he was already. Afraid that in the languid aftermath of sleepy passion she might reveal more than was healthy for her. As long as she withheld the totality of her need Claudia felt reasonably safe. If she was independent and slightly aloof then she kept him off-balance, and had a better chance of sustaining the interest of a man who thrived on challenge.

Last night he had fallen asleep in her arms after making love to her for hours and she had made the mistake of thinking that she could lie awake for a while, just holding him, enjoying a brief pretence of ownership of the hard body that was relaxed and vulnerable in sleep.

Of course, she had fallen asleep too and paid the price for it when she had woken just before dawn to the skilled caress of his hands and mouth and seen the sensual triumph in his expression. She had roused instinctively to his touch and been helpless to prevent her swift response, even as she realised the reason for his flagrant complacency. In staying he had broken her unspoken rule and, judging from his arrogant self-satisfaction when they finally rose, he had done it deliberately—shown her that there were no rules to this relationship but what she was prepared to speak out loud, and thus provide him with the opportunity to challenge.

'*You* may be able to take your time wandering in to work in the mornings, but you forget that *I'm* only an employee,' she said pointedly, still unwilling to concede his sly victory. 'Mornings are usually a rush for me. I don't have time to... to...'

'Enjoy a leisurely wake-up call? That's why I woke you before your alarm went off.' His grin was boldly unrepentant as he made short work of the bacon and eggs. 'Didn't you notice bells going off at a critical moment or does my lovemaking always ring peals over your head? I thought I had everything very nicely timed. In fact, if you don't sit down and relax for a few minutes you're going to be *early* for work. Don't worry about the dishes, I'll clean up. Aren't you going to have more than a piece of toast?' he added reprovingly as she reluctantly took his advice.

Now he was trying to manage her diet as well as her sleeping habits. Claudia's folly rose up to haunt her. Did she really want to give this dominating man house-room in her life despite the agonies he caused her? Unfortunately the answer was *yes*!

'It's all I ever have in the morning.'

'But now you're going to need to supplement your normal diet. You should be having cereal and milk and maybe some fresh fruit.'

'I have a perfectly balanced diet, thank you,' she said tartly. 'Besides, I'm not pregnant yet.'

'How do you know?'

She could feel herself blushing and concentrated fiercely on spreading marmalade on her toast. 'The usual way.'

There was a small, crackling silence. 'This morning?'

She knew that if she put the piece of toast she was toying with into her mouth she would choke.

'Yes.' She took a sip of coffee instead and burnt her mouth. She didn't know whether she was pleased or sorry that pregnancy wasn't even a possibility yet. Now, if he wanted to back out, she had given him the perfect opportunity!

'You should have said something...were you feeling uncomfortable? For God's sake, Claudia, I'm not an insatiable sex fiend, you know, you can refuse me whenever you want to...'

His voice was such an aggressive mixture of awkwardness and annoyance that she was jolted to look at him and as she did so his hard face began to tinge with unmistakable colour. Claudia's own embarrassment was forgotten as she realised that *he* was the one blushing for a change! Her fears that his first reaction would be relief subsided in a fierce surge of joy.

'I'm so glad to hear it,' she said, watching his colour deepen.

'You could have said you had a headache or something if you didn't feel like making love,' he muttered, clearly on the unaccustomed defensive.

Revelling in the moment, she raised her eyebrows and made the mistake of saying haughtily, 'Euphemisms, Morgan? I didn't think you were the kind of person who liked to have the bald facts cloaked in polite phrases.'

'I don't, but I thought you might. So why didn't you just tell me that you had your period and didn't want to make love?'

On the verge of taking another sip of the cooling coffee, she almost choked. Damn him for being so impossibly blunt! 'I didn't know until I had my shower.'

Another mistake. His high colour faded, a shiver of sensuous curiosity entered his eyes. 'And because you *did* want to make love...my instincts didn't fail me there, did they? So what is this about? Are you trying to find out my feelings on the subject? Are you expecting me to tell you that I won't be around until you make yourself sexually available again?'

'Morgan——'

'Because if you are, Claudia, you're being very insulting, to me and to yourself. I told you at the outset that this wasn't going to be a calendar-driven affair. Whatever time of the month it is makes no difference to me. If you don't want us to make love for the next few days we can still spend time together, and still enjoy a pleasurable degree of physical closeness...'

Somehow she didn't think he was talking about just holding hands. Stricken with a feverish shyness, Claudia stumbled into speech. 'I didn't mean to——'

'Good.' He picked up his cup with an irritating smugness. 'That's settled, then.' He took a taste and grimaced. 'Is this coffee instant?'

He looked down his wrinkled nose at it and his endearing expression of woe was such that she had to fight the urge to lean across and kiss him.

'If you don't like it you know what you can do. You're quite welcome to *uninvite* yourself to breakfast!' she crisped instead.

'I shall obviously have to buy you a percolator and show you how to make real coffee,' he said, looking amused by her pettishness.

'If I think it's worth having a percolator I'll buy my own,' she told him, her brown eyes snapping.

'Then I'll have to make sure you think it's worth it,' he murmured creamily. 'Why are we arguing over these minor details, Claudia? Did you think it would take my mind off the major ones? Like what you're going to do when you finally *do* get pregnant?'

Finally. He made it sound as if it was a difficult assignment that was going to take a long time. For a fleeting instant the evil thought flitted across her mind that, if she was very, very careful, she could stretch her time with him into months and months...

Shocked that such wickedness would even occur to her, Claudia punished her hopelessly compromised honour by taunting herself with the impossible.

'Why, give up my job and move in with you until the baby's born, of course,' she told him brazenly. 'You did offer to provide me with any support I needed and since I'm going to be bearing the entire physical burden of carrying your child it's only fair that you do your part by carrying the entire financial burden. After all, it seems the most practical thing to do.'

Her mockery fell flat. Morgan didn't blanch at the prospect of the invasion of his privacy, as she had fully expected him to do.

'I agree.'

'You agree?' For a moment the succinct answer confused her. Then it hit her. 'You *agree*?'

'I think it's an excellent idea.' His low, measured tone was in stark contrast to her startled squeak. He leaned back in his chair, the edges of his shirt falling away from the strongly muscled chest, a wild distraction to her senses that she desperately tried, and failed, to ignore.

Last night—and this morning—those muscles had been savagely sculpted under their smooth covering of skin as he moved around her, over her, in her, the male torso bunching and releasing with each driving thrust, flesh oiled with the sweat of his heated arousal, rigid and slippery to her questing touch. In repose the muscles flexed slowly, and with each steady rise and fall of his chest Claudia remembered the way that the air shuddered unsteadily in his lungs when he was deep in the grip of intense passion, his elegantly erotic murmurings degenerating into thick, involuntary grunts of uncontrollable pleasure as he approached his peak, instinctively trying to withhold his frenzied release until she could join him. And when he reached it the shout of raw, articulate triumph that accompanied his violent convulsions: her name...always her name, an acknowledgment of the extent, and the limits, of her power over Morgan. In bed there was no future and no past...no fear of failure, of betrayal, of pain...

'But why wait until you're pregnant?' he continued when she merely stood, staring abstractly at him amid the traitorous turmoil of her thoughts. 'Why not move in now?'

'Move in?' she parroted in shrill disbelief as she was jolted out of her distraction. 'With *you*? You mean—*live* with you?'

She sounded so incredulous that his unshaven jaw shifted, manoeuvring his mouth into a thinly uncompromising line as he hammered out his usual impeccable logic.

'Why not? It seems even more practical than your idea. Not only does it solve the problem of—er—immediate accessibility at critical points during your cycle, but it will also give you time to settle in and establish a comfortable routine before your hormones start rampaging. If you lived with me you wouldn't have to worry about paying rent or buying groceries, or the drudgery of housework...you wouldn't even have to work at all.

'Think of the advantages. Your job is quite a stressful and demanding one. Sure, you enjoy it, but it requires a consistently high level of energy and enthusiasm that puts you under considerable pressure to perform. I've seen you at work. You're meticulous to a fault. You forget to eat when you're busy and your mind is always leaping ahead to anticipate the next problem. I've been there and, believe me, the rewards of constantly out-performing yourself are not all they're cracked up to be. If you gave it up you'd much improve your chances of early conception. I'd make sure you had all the material comforts and the independence of an assured income. You'd be eating regular, healthy, home-cooked meals and getting plenty of rest and relaxation...'

Twenty minutes later Claudia stood staring at the apartment door that had just closed behind him with a smug click, holding her hand against her pounding chest and feeling as though she had swallowed a whirlwind.

The air buffeted in and out of her lungs as she struggled to comprehend what she had just allowed to happen.

She had been so *sure* that he was bluffing!

The fist of hot, red rage that had bunched in her throat when she first realised that he was offering to *pay* her for her exclusive services as a live-in mistress had choked off her outburst of fury just long enough for her see the glaring obviousness of the trap.

Losing her temper was precisely what the arrogant beast wanted! He *expected* her to turn down his in-sulting offer, just as she had fully expected him to turn down her meretricious demand. His revenge was a double-bluff, designed to goad her into a reckless re-sponse that would tell him what she was really feeling.

Instead pride had stiffened her spine, tamped down her bristling fury and called his stupid bluff.

But he hadn't thrown in his hand. Oh, no—he had raised the stakes still further and she, like a foolishly addicted gambler, had defiantly accepted the bet. If he wanted to pay for a love that was freely given, then that was his mistake!

Claudia forced herself to finish getting ready for work, her hands shaking so much that it took three tries to get her lipstick on. She must be mad, she told her pale reflection in the mirror. She must have the survival instincts of a lemming! Falling in love with Morgan Stone was bad enough, but lying to him and agreeing to have his child and moving in with him to live the lie every day was sheer insanity. What on earth did she think she was doing?

The same question was demanded of her a few hours later, by a stunned Simon Moore as he fingered her hastily typed resignation.

'But Claudia, I thought you were happy here!' he uttered in amazement. 'What about the Sports Five Hundred. The whole thing is just about to come together and most of the credit is yours. It's been your baby from the start!'

Claudia winced at the unconscious aptness of his phrasing. 'I have a month's notice to work out according to my contract,' she pointed out huskily, 'so I'll still be here during and for a few days after the race...unless you find someone to replace me sooner...'

Simon frowned, tapping an impatient hand on his desk. 'It's more likely to take longer—and that's fact, not flattery. You still haven't told me why.'

'It's—it's a personal matter,' said Claudia uncomfortably, conscious that he had every right to feel let down by her sudden decision to abandon her blossoming career. 'I really have enjoyed working here...it's just that, well, there are other things happening in my life right now that I want to concentrate on...'

'Have you won a lottery or come into some kind inheritance...' He paused delicately.

'Oh, no, nothing like that.' It was cowardly but she
was reluctant to tell Simon about something she could
hardly believe herself, even though she knew he would
find out soon enough—as would the whole world!

Morgan had phoned her soon after she had arrived at
work, not to whisper the lover-like reassurances that her
aching heart craved, but to inform her that he had decided to forestall the inevitable wild speculation over her
move into his home by ringing a journalist friend and
giving him the 'scoop' on their new relationship.

She was dumbfounded to realise that he was telling
her this after the fact. 'But I didn't agree——'

'You said you'd leave the details to me,' he interrupted smoothly. 'However much we might like to ignore
it, I'm news. Being frank at the outset will short-circuit
the gossip. You know yourself that the more you try to
avoid the Press, the more interested they become. If we
show we've got nothing to hide then they'll probably
settle for a routine raid on their background files to
support the story instead of trying to dig up any new
angles.'

Crushed by the avalanche of strategic logic, Claudia
floundered. 'But——'

'What's the matter? Frightened you might not be able
to back out now it's official?' he asked, his voice silky
with provocation. 'You could, but not gracefully, I'm
afraid. The Press would have a field day if you moved
out on me before you'd even moved it! They'd insist on
ferreting out the reason and you know what reporters
are like when they sniff a scandal...'

How dared he refer to her painful past with such
cheerful insouciance? 'Is that all you have to tell me?'
she asked stiffly, resisting the temptation to fling the
telephone across the room.

He didn't sound afraid at all. He sounded insufferably pleased with himself while she felt buffeted and bullied. She was doing exactly what she wanted desperately to do so why this inexplicable desire to burst into tears?

'Yes,' he lied with flagrant aplomb. 'Except for the fact that I've also arranged for a removal company to help you shift your things this evening. It shouldn't take long, given that you've hardly had time to acquire any furniture of your own. I'd collect you myself but I have a late meeting so I'll have a car delivered to the apartment so that you can drive yourself to the house. I'll see you at home at about eight for dinner—call my housekeeper and let her know if you have any preferences. All right?'

He was too quick for her. He hung up before she had a chance to slam the receiver down on him. He certainly wasn't leaving anything to chance, or giving her much time for first, let alone second thoughts! Everything was happening so fast. Claudia had an awful sense of fate rushing at breakneck speed towards her instead of meekly waiting for her to take her chosen path.

'I'll probably do a bit of freelance PR work if there's any available,' Claudia added hastily now as Simon continued to regard her with a deeply concerned frown.

That had been Morgan's idea, too, as he had taken advantage of the stunned silence that had followed his bombshell in the kitchen. He had murmured that, of course, if living with him turned out to be *too* restful and unexciting, then she was welcome to experiment with his fearsome array of computer technology and set up a home office for herself. The smouldering gleam in his eye when he had said it implied that excitement would be the very last thing her life with him would lack. Given the upheavals of the past few weeks, she could well believe it!

Simon's mouth compressed. 'I can't promise any-thing, Claudia. You know we handle most of our business in-house.'

'Oh, I wasn't suggesting that.' She flushed awkwardly at the subtle reproof. 'I mean, if you wouldn't mind giving me a reference...'

He had agreed, not without some reservations for which Claudia couldn't blame him. Discretion was Simon's watchword but she knew that if she told him that her new career was to be Morgan Stone's live-in mistress he would probably feel obligated to warn her of her extreme folly. She didn't need a lecture on the subject; she was already intimately acquainted with it.

The fact that she knew no one in Wellington inti-mately enough to discuss her feelings with made her feel isolated and yet also, in a strange way, safe. Her aloneness insulated her from the personal consequences of her actions for there was no one else to consider but herself, no one to be hurt that she chose to follow her heart, rather than the dictates of common sense and conscience. Certainly she would have to put up with being in the public eye again for a while, and suffer the sidelong glances and gossip of colleagues while she worked out her notice, but she could cope with that as long as she knew that there was Morgan to go home to at night...

And to go home in she had her shiny new toy!

She had quite forgotten Morgan's mention of a car and when the ornately enamelled Morgan key-ring was hand-delivered to her door that same evening Claudia forced herself to wait until the removal men had left with the final box of her miscellaneous possessions and she had packed up the last of her clothes before she went downstairs to see what kind of car he had lent her.

Instead of the modest compact she had anticipated, there, parked on the street and already drawing interest from evening strollers along the waterfront, was the very same royal blue Greenwood Corvette that Claudia had admired on her first visit to his showroom.

At first she thought that she was suffering delusions of grandeur, and she sat gingerly in the driver's seat for several minutes before she looked in the glove compartment for the letter that the employee who had delivered the car had said was there. Sure enough, there was an envelope with the elegant Morgan and Son logo embossed on the flap and her name printed on the front in a very definite, slashing hand.

If she hadn't been in love with Morgan already she would have fallen irrevocably when she read the provocative note that was wrapped around the ownership papers. Her pride might have balked at the outrageous extravagance of his gift but her heart melted at the words that told her that price hadn't entered the equation. The choice had been a piece of whimsy she was helpless to deny him. He wrote simply.

> Whenever I look at this car now, I think of you. I can't imagine anyone else owning it and it's playing havoc with my concentration. A sexy car, for a very sexy lady. Enjoy.

She did. Shamelessly.

At first tentative and uncertain, she was determined to overcome her fear and she soon got the hang of handling such a powerful car, zipping back and forth along Marine Drive every day, discovering for herself the extraordinarily seductive allure of driving a superbly crafted machine. Behind the wheel she gained her first real understanding of the obsession that had consumed Chris, although a ticket for speeding on her fourth outing curbed any desire for recklessness. She saved that for her behaviour off the road!

In fact, her first few weeks of adjusting to being publicly viewed as Morgan Stone's resident woman proved less difficult than she had feared. Envy rather than condemnation seemed the general response. For one thing, to Morgan's amusement and Claudia's chagrin, her exotic car drew more Press attention than the personal aspects of their relationship. The most provocative piece of speculation was a risible suggestion that Morgan had provided Claudia with the Corvette so that she could drive it in the Sports Five Hundred. Reading that particular rumour had wiped the smug smile off Morgan's face and he had scotched it with his friendly sources with considerably less than his usual good humour.

For those few weeks she lived safe within a fragile bubble of perfect happiness, cherishing each unfolding day as a gift more precious and unique than any other that Morgan had bestowed upon her. She was hectically busy in her job as the date of the race neared and secretly resented every moment that nine-to-five reality stole from her beautiful fantasy life with Morgan. It couldn't go on forever, of course, this defiantly carefree existence, and one afternoon, arriving home much earlier than usual because she wanted to make use of Morgan's sophisticated desk-top publishing program to produce what would probably be her last publicity layout for the hotel, Claudia's glorious bubble burst.

Entering the master bedroom she shared with Morgan, she shed her jacket and began to unbutton her blouse, her mouth curving sensuously as she debated which dress she might welcome Morgan home in. Since he worked more flexible hours than she did, he was usually home first, and she looked forward to the prospect of surprising him. The element of surprise, she felt, would be an important factor in retaining his interest once the novelty of their relationship wore off.

At that moment Mark walked out of the *en-suite* bathroom and Claudia froze, the blood running up into her face at the look of stunned condemnation on his handsome face.

'They told me, but I didn't believe it,' he said jerkily, in hoarse tones of shock. 'I really thought it was just someone's stupid idea of a tasteless joke. But it's true, isn't it? You're living here. You're sleeping with him ...'

'I——' Claudia moved her hands helplessly. He had obviously drawn his own conclusions from the half-open wardrobe and the cosy clutter of cosmetics next to his father's cologne and shaving kit on the bathroom shelf.

'I didn't realise you were going to be back so soon,' she said inanely. 'M—— Your father said you were going to spend another few weeks in Europe on holiday...'

'You mean this is only a temporary thing? Were you going to move out before I came back so I wouldn't know what was going on?' he asked brutally.

'*No!*' With a wave of horror she realised she hadn't even thought about the complications that would ensue when Mark returned. In her blind grab at happiness she had allowed herself to forget he even existed. 'We—I— I've only been here a few weeks... It sort of just...*happened*,' she explained, her shaking hands trying frantically to rebutton her blouse.

'Nothing ever *just happens* as far as my father is concerned,' Mark cracked out, looking suddenly older than his years and very much a product of his genes. 'He always has a very good reason for everything he does.' He looked around the room as if he had never seen it before, turning back to her to burst out, 'For God's sake, I've scarcely been gone more than a month! When I left you didn't even know each other, much less *like* each other!'

'I wouldn't put it quite like that——' she protested weakly, clenching her hands over her roiling stomach. If Morgan had to choose between his son and his mistress she was wretchedly aware of who the loser would be.

'Then how *would* you put it?' he demanded crudely, backing her nervously against the bed. 'He's never actually moved one of his women in here before so I guess you must really have the hots for each other. Can't do without it at least once a day, huh? Or, knowing my Dad's mania for thoroughness——'

'*Mark*——!' Claudia was absolutely scarlet by this time. Mark had the grace to look slightly ashamed as he raked his hand through his hair and turned away.

'I used to think you were so...' He slashed the air with an expressive gesture as he paced away from her again in disgust. 'How *could* you, Claudia? For God's sake, he's old enough——'

'If you say he's old enough to be my father, I'll clock you one,' said Claudia, striving to regain her equilibrium with forced humour. 'For a start it's not true. He's *your* father, Mark, not mine. To me he's a mature, intelligent and...very exciting man.' Her voice thickened on the last words and Mark swung back to look at her, the hostility in his hazel eyes muted by curiosity. She perched weakly on the edge of the bed.

'But—*Dad*? I told you what he was like. Women are just another convenient form of relaxation, he *never* gets seriously involved. After all the agonies you went through with Chris I can't believe you'd let yourself be sucked into another situation like this. What security have you got now? When I spoke to your friend on the switchboard she said you'd even given up your job!' His look of horror was almost comical.

'I can always get another job, Mark.'

'What on earth have you let him *do* to you?' He sat heavily down on the bed beside her, trying to read her answer in her strained face.

'Nothing,' she murmured, her eyes as wise as they were unknowingly wistful. 'I've done it all to myself.'

The little she said was far too much. He sucked in a breath. 'Oh, my God—you're in love with him!' He sounded even more horrified than ever. 'Oh, Claudia, you *fool*!' His fingers tightened on hers as he asked quietly. 'How long do you think it's going to last?'

'It doesn't matter.' She shrugged, holding her head high. She mustn't let him think that she had any regrets, or blame his father for not being the man she wanted him to be.

'Yes, it does,' he said roughly, letting go her hands in order to pull her limp body close and hug her until her throat ached with unshed tears. Pulling back, his eyes fell to her unevenly buttoned blouse. He sighed, and began to match them up properly, with the brisk resignation of a parent tidying up an unruly child, and Claudia knew it was going to be all right. She was forgiven. 'Oh, Claudia, if you had to fall in love why couldn't it have been with someone who wouldn't ride roughshod over your feelings? Why in hell couldn't you have fallen in love with *me*?'

His arrogance was almost enough to make her smile. 'Because you're not in love with me.'

'Neither is he.'

The wounding words were spoken before he could call them back and as if he could apologise for their cruel truth Mark stilled his fumbling with her blouse and leaned forward to kissed her gently, passionlessly, on her trembling mouth.

Seconds later Claudia was staring into murderous blue eyes, a desperate shield between father and son as Morgan strode through the door.

CHAPTER TEN

'TAKE your hands off her!'

Mark, who had put his hands on Claudia's shoulders to steady her as they both guiltily jumped up from the bed, tightened them in automatic repudiation of his father's blistering order while she rushed into speech, gabbling out her reasons for being home early.

At her back Mark remained silent but his silence, like his hands on her shoulders, was a kind of clear physical taunt.

'And when I walked in,' Claudia finished awkwardly, 'I found Mark was home——'

'So I see.' The slowly enunciated words sent an icy chill down Claudia's spine as she stood nervously between the two men. Morgan prowled closer, bringing with him a strong aura of menace.

'I wondered why you had left the office again in such a rush,' he charged his son broodingly. 'Irene said that she told you I was across in the showroom. She thought it rather strange that you should take the trouble to call in on your way from the airport and yet not even bother to stay and say hello...'

'But *you* obviously didn't.' Mark's voice was as accusing as his father's. 'You knew exactly where I'd gone!'

Morgan stilled, his big shoulders flexing dangerously under his dark jacket. The two men were dressed in very similar business suits and Claudia felt like the tender meat in a brutally stylish sandwich.

'Why didn't you let us know that you'd moved your flight forward a week?' Morgan demanded bluntly.

A week? Claudia swallowed. Why hadn't he mentioned Mark's imminent return if he had known about it? Had he intended, as Mark had claimed, to be rid of her before then?

'I thought I'd surprise you.' The murmur that stirred the hair on the back of Claudia's neck was supremely sarcastic. 'Instead, *I* was the one who got the big surprise.'

'I told you to take your hands off her.' Morgan's terse command was no longer an order, it was pure threat.

'Morgan, we were just *talking*——'

'Oh, is that what you're calling it now?' he interrupted Claudia with lethally soft sarcasm, reaching out a hand to toy suggestively with a button that Mark had failed to restore to its rightful place. Claudia shivered.

'I—I was changing——'

'Into something more comfortable... for Mark?'

'No, of course not,' she denied the silky suggestion frantically. 'He—I—we had no idea we were even going to see each other...'

'You're stuttering, Claudia. Are you nervous?'

'Of course she's nervous, with you standing over her like some brooding great tyrant!' Mark said angrily. 'What's the matter with you? Back off, why don't you?'

'Why don't *you*?'

Helplessly Claudia watched as the hand insistently nudging her button splayed flat in the air in front of her then curled into a savage fist.

'No, Morgan, don't——' She put both hands out and wrapped them protectively around the fist. She wouldn't be responsible for another angry estrangement between the two!

'Don't what? Give the boy what he wants?' he asked rawly.

'Don't be silly. This isn't what you think——'

'Mark *wasn't* kissing and undressing you on the bed? My bed? *Our* bed?' The blue eyes grew hotter, the voice thicker with each violent syllable.

Oh, God! Claudia felt Mark stiffen behind her, his hands pressing even more deeply on to her shoulders. 'He was just being kind——'

'The hell he was!' With a gasp Claudia felt the fist move, powering out of her grasp, but instead of lashing past her it hooked around, spinning her out from under Mark's charge and dragging her back against him as he backed away, his other arm left free as a potential weapon.

'Damn you——!'

'No, Mark, don't——' Claudia held up shaking hands to stop him as he stepped aggressively forward. 'For goodness' sake, Morgan,' she pleaded to the man whose hostage she now was, 'think about what you're doing——'

'I know exactly what I'm doing. I'm making it very clear to everyone where they stand. You may have her friendship, Mark, but everything else is mine. She's mine.'

To illustrate the fact Morgan's free hand moved over her blouse, to find and cup her breast in a gesture that was as possessive as it was explicit.

Claudia tipped back her head to protest and found her mouth smothered with a ravishing, open-mouthed kiss that was every bit as explicit as the hand on her breast. He took his time and she was flushed with excitement and furiously embarrassed by the time he lifted his head.

After giving her one look of savage satisfaction Morgan focused his will again on his son. 'We've been lovers for weeks,' he said harshly. 'Accept it. Any hopes you had in her direction are dead and buried.'

His evident jealousy sent a wave of hope crashing over Claudia, quickly swamped by the despairing realisation that it was a purely sexual possessiveness.

'Claudia?' Mark's bewildered request made her gaoler shake her roughly within the prison of his arms.

'Go on, Duchess,' he ordered grimly. 'Tell him how much you enjoy my lovemaking. Tell him that this wasn't a one-sided seduction. Tell him that I'm the most important man in your life for the foreseeable future——'

In the ensuing, deadly silence Mark suddenly seemed to relax as he studied his father's stubborn belligerence. 'Why don't you let her go? You're hurting her.'

'No, I'm not. Am I, Duchess?' Without loosening his grip Morgan turned her tightly in his arms so that she was looking warily up at him. 'She likes me to be an aggressive lover.' He fitted his mouth over hers again, this time with lavish care. He kissed her with his whole body, tucking her intimately between his legs, his fingers splayed across her rounded buttocks and massaging them sensuously, uncaring of their deeply intrigued audience.

'Are we still having this conversation, or am I supposed to make my excuses and leave?' said Mark wryly, when it appeared that the other two had forgotten about him.

'Good idea,' said Morgan thickly, breaking off the kiss with extreme reluctance. 'Shut the door on your way out.'

'Morgan!' Claudia tried to squirm out of his seductive embrace but, feeling the familiar hardness stirring against her thighs, subsided blushingly. 'Mark—I'm sorry...'

'For what? Chosing a decrepit old man over a young and virile one?' He grinned. 'That's OK, honey. If you change your mind, you know where to find me.'

In the circumstances Claudia thought his flippancy dangerously misplaced, but Morgan didn't. His cynical smile was every bit as amused as Mark's cheeky one and infinitely more masculine.

'Stay away from her, son, if you value that virile, young hide.'

'Well, now, that's going to be fairly difficult to do,' Mark pointed out slyly. 'I live here, too, remember? Won't it be fun, the three of us in a ménage à trois...?' Wickedly he picked up Claudia's limp hand and raised it to his mouth.

'Mark——'

Claudia's warning was ignored.

'Come on, Dad, you've never quibbled at the idea of sharing before.'

Claudia's eyes widened with shock at the implications of that one, but Morgan was quick to counteract the mischief. 'Since we've never shared the same taste in women the idea was never any threat to my ageing masculinity,' he drawled pointedly, 'and, even if it had been, I never cared sufficiently to worry about it...'

'But with Claudia it's different?'

Claudia held her breath. She knew what Mark was trying to do with his clumsy probing. He was trying to help. But she would far rather he didn't stir up trouble...

'With Claudia the question doesn't arise. I think even your eager virility might draw the line at taking your pregnant stepmother for a lover.'

'Pregnant? *Stepmother*?' Mark looked pole-axed, as well he might!

'Didn't Claudia tell you while you were so busily...*talking* that she's decided to have my baby?'

Claudia, too, was stunned at the lengths to which he was prepared to go to cut his son out of her life.

'You're pregnant?' Mark's eyes fell to her flat stomach and then jerked frowningly to his father. 'You married her because she's pregnant!'

'I do seem to be making a habit of shotgun marriages, don't I?' Morgan drawled, unruffled by the suggestion, his glibness catapulting Claudia out of her state of suspended animation.

'*Stop* it! *Both* of you,' she demanded hectically. 'This is absolutely ridiculous! You can stop looking so appalled, Mark, of course we're not married.' She spat out the word as if it tasted vile.

'But we will be, by the time the baby's born,' Morgan said smoothly.

Claudia sucked in a cry as she wrenched herself out of his arms, pain and anger cutting deep into her heart. 'We don't even know if there is a baby!'

'Is that a no?' he asked evenly. 'Think before you speak, Claudia, because I don't take rejection very well. I might not ask again.'

'You call this asking?' she choked.

'You want me to grovel for the privilege of making an honest woman out of you?' he had the gall to say coolly.

Her narrowed eyes glittered with golden spears of contempt. He wouldn't know honesty if it hit him over the head! 'The idea of having your face at boot-level has a very definite appeal at the moment,' she told him fiercely.

His eyes smouldered hotly in response. 'Or I could just throw you on that bed and strip you,' he threatened silkily. 'You never say no to anything I want there. Hell, a few minutes of foreplay and you're usually the one begging . . .'

'Er—Dad——'

Morgan didn't even look at him. His goading challenge was all directed at Claudia's scarlet face.

'Get out of here, Mark. This doesn't concern you. Well, Claudia, make your choice.'

'You mean you're actually offering me one?' she sneered, conscious of the deliciously familiar tension beginning to stretch inside her.

'Maybe I will go back to the office for a while,' murmured Mark gleefully as he edged out of the door. 'Er—congratulations, by the way...'

'How dare you imply that I'm so promiscuous that I'd carry on a sleazy affair behind your back with anyone who asked me, let alone Mark?' Claudia continued on the attack, only to gasp in shock as Morgan picked her up and tossed her effortlessly on to the bed, exactly as he had threatened. Fearful excitement raced through her veins as she remembered the next part of his erotic threat. 'Don't think you can——!'

The air puffed out of her as he came down heavily on top of her. Even fully dressed the contact was shockingly electric, shorting out her anger as he completed the live circuit with his wandering hands, pulling at her clothes and his own until they were both breathlessly naked and aggressively aroused.

'Don't think that this proves anything,' Claudia moaned as he gripped her strongly, shifting up and over her, parting her thighs and moving insistently between them, teasing her moist heat with his swollen body, withholding the fullness of him until she clutched at his hips with reckless impatience.

'It proves that you forgive me.' His tongue probed against a stiffened nipple as he deliberately aimed all the weapons in his sexual arsenal on his unresisting target.

'Forgive you... for... what...?' she laboured to remember.

'Anything...' He licked her nipple again. 'Everything...' He began to suckle with noisy intensity, at the same instant allowing her to pull him gloriously deep inside her, the satisfaction only fleeting as he slowly withdrew, to thrust even more deeply than before. The thick sounds of descriptive pleasure he made as he worked rhythmically over her sent tiny vibrating shocks thrilling through her moistly conductive flesh, slowly building to a powerful erotic pulsing that only he could transfer into the exquisite moment of perfect completion.

'Yes...oh, yes!' she whispered as she threw herself into the delirium of unrestrained loving.

'You forgive me for my unreasonable jealousy...?'

If she had been in her right mind she would have been delighted to hear him beg but as it was the words could no longer satisfy her. She welcomed the completeness of his possession. 'Yes...yes...'

'You're mine,' he rasped, the muscles in his arms cording with agonised tension as he supported himself over her writhing body, driving her harder, deeper into a sustained frenzy. 'Say yes, dammit, tell me you want to do this with me every day of your life...'

'Yes, yes, *yes*...!' she sobbed, and the explosive reaction that was her reward tumbled her into sweet oblivion.

When she woke, hours later, Morgan was gone. On the bedside table was the only proof, apart from her sweetly aching body, that it had not all been some wild and erotic dream.

Had to go back to work. Don't believe in long engagements, especially in our case. I'll organise the licence, the trappings are up to you...

What made her heart tremble was not the written confirmation that his proposal had been real and not just the mockery of his jealous possession, but the casual signature.

Love, Morgan.

Love?

In all the passionate words that had passed between them, love had been the only taboo.

But if it were true...?

She would sell her soul if it were true! Morgan had no need to marry her. Marriage would make him vulnerable, give her a public and private power over him which as his mistress she could never hope to achieve. So why would a rich, successful, attractive and powerful man such as Morgan risk the emotional and financial exploitation? Unless...

Love, Morgan.

Claudia stared at the two words, her thoughts in a turmoil of anguished uncertainty. Her time had run out.

She rose and dressed swiftly, anxious for it to be over. If Morgan still wanted to marry her after she had told him about the reasons for her baby's death, well, she would know then that he *did* love her, with a strength that would last a lifetime.

She drove carefully, rehearsing her speech all the way, trying out the best phrases, cringing at the knowledge that there was no way she could soften the brutal impact of her confession.

At Morgan's office she was relieved when his secretary waved her in with a conspiratorial smile, not even bothering to check with her boss. After today there might not be too many more smiles coming her way around here.

He was sitting in his swivel chair facing away from the door, studying a slim file on his lap. Claudia hesitated in the doorway.

'Morgan?'

He froze, his head lifting like an animal scenting prey, but he didn't turn. Claudia stepped inside the office and closed the door, thankful for its cool support at her back. Without it she thought her knees might not hold her upright. She moistened her lips, frantically trying to remember her opening line.

'Morgan, I need to——'

'You *bitch*!' He came out of his chair and round the desk in a single stride. 'You sadistic, calculating, vindictive *bitch*!'

Stunned by his violently premature reaction, Claudia could only stand helpless and white-faced as he attacked her with his fury.

'Oh, yes, you might well look sick, you little——' He used a word which made her flush violently, then pale again as he continued with coruscating contempt, 'You are sick. You should be bloody well locked away! You let me believe that I was responsible for the *death of a child*!'

Claudia's mind went blank, all her careful defences devastated by the realisation that he already knew what she had agonised over telling him. Once again, she had failed him.

'What in the *hell* did you hope to achieve?' he ripped at her with white-lipped disgust. '*Revenge*? For what? Hurt pride? You admitted you never wanted Mark anyway so don't tell me I deprived you of your heart's desire. I was never a person to you at all, was I? I was an object, a convenient whipping post. You used me then, you bitch, to deny your own responsibility and you're still trying to use me!'

He towered over her, his remorseless fury battering her with a force that made his earlier display of temper a passing frown in comparison.

'And my God—what about this new child you professed to want from me?' he ground out pitilessly. 'Was that going to be just another pawn in your macabre game of "let's make Morgan suffer"? Or maybe there was never going to be a child. Maybe that was going to be your way of drawing out my guilt, torturing me with something you knew I'd never have. Well, you can rot in hell before I play any more part in your sick fantasies. Do you hear me, Claudia? You can rot in *hell*!'

And with that he threw the folder he was holding in her stricken face and walked away, sweeping a chair violently out of his path on his way. The cardboard file fell to the ground, papers fluttering out of it and she bent to pick it up, her body functioning purely on automatic. Her crabbed fingers stilled as she realised what it was she was gathering up.

'This is my medical file from the hospital...'

She had only whispered but he heard. He spun on his heel, visibly restraining himself from further violence.

'How did you get it?' she asked numbly. She had never dreamed he would find out this way, through cold, clinical details. 'I thought doctors didn't release this sort of information——'

'Yes, another amusing twist for your little tale of revenge,' he snarled, his fists clenched at his side as if he was fighting the temptation to use them on her. 'You'll laugh at this: I pulled some strings. I thought it might help for me to know... what sort of problems you might have bearing my child. I didn't want to put you through the trauma of trying if there was no possibility of carrying to term——'

Oh, God, he *had* loved her... 'But I told you——'

'You told me a lot of things, Claudia.' He cut her off with an angry swipe that deliberately sent a pen set crashing off his desk. Like the overturned chair it seemed symbolic of the devastation her lies had wrought. 'None of them worth sh——'

'Morgan, that's why I'm here. I came to tell you——'

'Did you?' he sneered cuttingly. 'How kind. What were you going to say? Hey, Morgan, guess what? You're not a murderer after all. I've been stringing you along all this time just for the pleasure of watching you squirm!'

The word *murderer* made her heart shrink to a tight knot in her chest. 'Morgan, please, won't you at least listen——?'

'To more lies? More self-serving half-truths?' he exploded, his eyes burning blue flames in a face that was a rictus of disgust. 'It was hard, but I could understand you lying about your baby's parentage. But this? *This*?' For a horrible moment he looked as if he was actually going to vomit but he swallowed the bile to utter harshly, 'I don't want to hear, Claudia. Not any of it. Get out! Get out of my office. Get out of my house. Get out of my *life*——'

'Morgan, I love you——' she began desperately and he swore, more vilely than before, smearing her with the taint of his violent loathing.

'Get out, Claudia, while you still can. If you don't then I won't be responsible for my actions. I could very easily kill you for what you've done to me——!'

Shaking, knowing that she had left it too late, that it had always been too late for them, Claudia turned, fumbling blindly for the elusive door-handle.

'And Claudia—you walk away from this relationship empty-handed. Understand? You take *nothing*!' He addressed her slender back with savage insolence. 'If you do I'll sue you for fraud and see you raped of every shred of reputation in open court. So leave the keys to the Corvette at the desk on your way out. You were a good lay but you didn't last long enough to earn the spare tyre, let alone the whole car!'

Claudia stiffened, goaded by the last, unforgivable insult into looking back over her shoulder at him with eyes that blazed with a rage that matched his. That car had been a symbol of their happiness together. She wouldn't let him take even her memories from her!

'Go to hell, Morgan Stone!'

She didn't remember the reckless drive back to the house on Marine Drive, only getting there in miraculously fast time and stumbling on her knees on the concrete drive as she fell out of the driver's door, her hand stinging with a burn from the hot tyre that she had momentarily propped herself against. She was still shaking like a leaf when she staggered into the house, automatically picking up the telephone in passing as it began to shrill upon her nerves.

'H-hello?'

A dead silence greeted her croaky greeting, then a guttural snarl. 'You're lucky to be alive, the way you took off from here!'

'You call this being alive?' she asked, with a hysterical sob of wretched black humour, and hung up on him.

She took the telephone upstairs with her, but he didn't ring back.

All night and for the next two days Morgan didn't ring. He didn't set foot in his own house, and Claudia didn't set foot out of it. She called the hotel and told them she had a virulent dose of summer flu and without a qualm diverted all her work to her replacement who had arrived from head office for his two-week familiarisation period.

Mark came home, crushing her with his concern and jabbing her with worried questions, but she wouldn't talk to him, couldn't explain the emotional numbness that smothered and protected her; could only sit and wait like a small, wounded animal in a trap, afraid to move, afraid to draw a predator's attention to itself...

On the third morning, before he reluctantly left for work, Mark finally pressed her more insistently, 'What are you going to do, Claudia? Dad's holed up at the hotel and blows a gasket at the mere mention of your name. You're sitting here like death warmed over. If...well, if you have to leave, where will you go?'

His worry pierced the thick grey envelope of her misery with a bright shaft of pain.

Leave Morgan?

She wondered if he knew she was still living in his house. No, if he had he would probably have hired some heavies to throw her out on the street by now.

'Go?' She didn't have anywhere to go, she realised in sudden panic. She couldn't stay at the HarbourPoint—her job there was nearly over and, besides, *he* was there. True to Mark's gloomy prediction of a few days ago she had managed to leave herself with nothing, *nobody* ...

The shaft widened to become a shining path through the self-pitying murk that had buried her natural resilience. Claudia's dull brown eyes gleamed with a spark of resistance. After everything she had risked to be with Morgan, why was she giving up on him with so little fight? She had seen the way he respected those who stood up to him, even when he believed they were in the wrong. She had done a very great wrong, yes, but even the most hardened criminals were given their day in court. Now that Morgan's temper had had a few days to cool, might she not be able to approach him on a more rational level?

Would a man who hated her have made that angry phone call after their row? she asked herself. He hadn't asked about the car, he had been checking up to make sure she had got home safely. Even then, in the grip of a molten fury that cursed her very existence, he had been concerned enough to make that call ...

What did she have to lose by confronting him again? She had nothing left to lose! But how, if he was so determined to avoid it? There had to be some way to lure him into a meeting. Her eyes narrowed as she suddenly remembered something he had threatened in the white-heat of the moment.

'Do you know any good lawyers, Mark?' she asked slowly.

He looked wary, startled by the sudden proud lift of her chin after several days of seeing it sunken on her chest. 'Sure. Why?'

Her eyes narrowed. 'I want to file an action for breach of promise.'

His jaw dropped. 'Breach of—— You mean ... *Dad*?'

'Nobody else has asked me to marry him lately,' she said grimly.

'But Claudia—my God, he'll never—my *God*!'

She refused to let his appalled jabber undermine the desperate act of a desperate woman. 'You were there,' she insisted. 'You heard him say he was going to marry me.'

Mark gulped. 'You want *me* to appear as your witness?' His voice squeaked like a girl's as he regarded her with awe. 'Claudia, he'd *kill* me—he'll kill us both!'

She looked at him with grave brown eyes that shimmered with the futile tears that she had refused to shed. 'Some things are worth dying for, aren't they?'

A grin of unholy amusement crawled slowly across his stunned expression as he contemplated her determined face.

'Yes. Yes, I guess they are. And I not only know a few good lawyers—some of them owe me favours. You just sit tight here, Claudia, and leave the fast-tracking to me!'

After he had gone, finding the whole thing far more entertaining than she thought was wise, or appropriate, Claudia allowed her confidence to collapse. Breach of promise? she thought sourly. That was a laugh! All that loving Morgan had ever promised her was heartache and he had delivered on that one with interest!

Having a vague idea that in the interest of profit lawyers always moved extremely slowly, Claudia consoled herself with the thought that she would have plenty of time to change her mind if her courage failed her. Meanwhile at least she could feel that she was making some attempt to take control of her life again.

For the first time in days she ate her breakfast and even managed a few nibbles of lunch, in deference to the despairing efforts of Morgan's very confused housekeeper.

In the afternoon, enervated by the heat and the effects of insomnia, Claudia smothered herself in sunscreen and sunbathed defiantly on the terrace in an effort to improve what she gloomily decided was her prison pallor.

A savage screech of tyres and the slam of a car door woke her from a light doze and she sat up woozily, aware of a painfully warm tingling in her skin and annoyed at herself for overdoing it. Was Mark home already? Checking to see she hadn't decided to slit her wrists? She really must tell him to stop hovering over her like a nervous parent. She got unsteadily to her feet and looked over the balcony, her eyes widening with horror as she saw the squat black car parked below, its tyres still smoking angrily.

At the same instant she heard her name echo through the house.

'Claudia? Claudia! I know you're here, Claudia, don't think you can hide from me!'

Frantically she looked around for something to put over her sleek yellow maillot but she hadn't brought her wrap out with her and she was contemplating snatching the tablecloth from under the remains of her alfresco lunch when Morgan exploded up the stairwell into the sunroom and saw her.

'I thought I told you to get out of my house,' he rapped out. His eyes smouldered over her exposed limbs as he stepped out on to the deck and something flicked in his eyes. 'You're expecting me, I see.'

The sardonic murmur was such an unexpected turnaround that Claudia flinched. 'Don't flatter yourself!' she snapped, controlling the urge to cross her hands over her heaving breasts.

He was shaven but managed to project an aura of unshaven haggardness, his eyes narrowed dauntingly in a face full of implacable straight lines. In a light grey three-piece suit and white shirt he made Claudia feel intimidatingly naked and ill-prepared.

'What else can a man think when he's so desirable women are driven to *court* his attention?' He tapped his palm with a tube of paper tied with ribbon.

'Do you know what happened to me today, Claudia?'

She shook her head helplessly, afraid to ask, mesmerised by the paper in his hand. Another medical file to beat her over the conscience with...?

'Two men—two very large, sullen-looking men accosted me in my showroom in the middle of an interview with a US Cable TV channel about the race...an interview that *you* helped set-up, incidentally...and served me with some legal papers which they were at pains to explain in very loud and explicit detail. Not only am I being sued for breach of promise, it seems, but my own son is apparently a willing witness against me and my own address is listed as the source of the complaint.'

'R-really?' Claudia didn't dare look him in the face. That lethal, silky soft evenness was totally unnerving. What on earth had Mark done? Even Claudia knew that no legal papers were ever drawn up this fast!

She watched through lowered lashes as the paper was unrolled by hands which bore ominously white knuckles. 'Now, what kind of woman do you suppose does something this stupid?'

A woman in love.

The silence stretched. Claudia swallowed. The warm tingling in her skin had become a scalding heat. To her horror she could feel his eyes crawling over her body again, and her breasts begin to swell and ache with remembered hunger.

She put her hands around her waist, unconsciously deepening the cleavage of the low-cut bathing suit as she jutted her jaw with an aggression to match his. 'An angry one?'

His hard, arrogant expression didn't change.

'Angry?' His voice was still as soft as the rest of him was hard. He reached out with the offending papers and scraped the edge of one corner tauntingly over the dark circle of her nipple revealed by the paleness of her costume. 'I don't think so, Claudia.' His nostrils flared as her nipple instantly contracted. 'You do know, don't you,' he said, scraping the paper slowly back and forth with cruel deliberation, 'that this breach of promise isn't worth the paper it's written on?'

Claudia trembled. 'Morgan, I——'

'Don't.' He stopped her with a clipped monosyllable. 'Don't lie to me. Not again. Not ever again!' Having slapped her in the face with breathless hope, he struck her again with another terse demand. 'Are you pregnant?'

'What?' She blinked at him, dazed.

'This suit, it mentions my abandonment of you in a . . . delicate condition . . .'

Oh, *Mark*!

She looked at him, clear-eyed, not even tempted. 'No.'

If he wanted her, it was going to be for herself, alone!

'How can you be so sure? Your period isn't due until next week.'

She would never, *never* get used to his crude frankness at the most delicate of moments. Blushing, Claudia caught at the paper that was teasing her breasts, crumpling it like the irrelevancy they both knew it was.

'I—I'm sure I'm probably not,' she said firmly.

'"Sure" and "probably" are a contradiction in terms.'

'Is that what you came here for, to talk terms?' she flared, stung by his cold formality.

'You called and I came,' he told her.

'I didn't——'

'Claudia, this suit is so much trash.' He illustrated his claim by taking it out of her nerveless fingers and throwing it over the balcony. 'It's a paste-up job, a mishmash of legalese that amounts to out-and-out blackmail. I don't know who your lawyer is but I'm going to see that he gets disbarred. And as for those two loud-mouthed goons he used as process servers——!'

'I—that was Mark...I only suggested it this morning— I wasn't really going to go through with it...' She didn't mean to cry, she really didn't, but his crookedly mocking smile was too much for her. 'I hate you,' she whispered as he gathered her against his chest.

'And I hate you.'

He kissed her, to show her how much, and the tears flowed even faster. Was this execution or absolution? She still didn't know.

'I'm sorry, I'm sorry, I'm sorry...' she murmured brokenly into his mouth. 'I was mad—you were right, I was temporarily insane when I lost the baby, but even when the insanity passed I was afraid to face what I'd done. I just wanted to forget it—all of it...' She shuddered with the memory. 'And...and then when we met again I was—I still couldn't make myself do it. I knew you would be disgusted—you were right to be, because there's no excuse. But I really was going to tell you that day...that was why I followed you to the office. I would never, ever have married you letting you think...'

'That I was a murderer of babies?'

'No, oh, no—don't say that...' She cupped his face and looked deep into his eyes, shocked to see that the glorious blue was veiled by rain-drenched clouds. 'I'm so sorry,' she repeated helplessly, aching for him. 'I'll never forgive myself. I—I'll understand if you can't either——'

His gaze held her wavering one steady. 'No, you won't.'

She bit her lip, caught out in yet another lie. 'I'll try to understand...I'll do anything you want to try and make it up to you...'

'Anything except go away and leave me in peace.'

His bitter irony was almost too much to bear. She closed her eyes. 'Even that...'

'And what if you really are pregnant?'

Oh, God, he was relentless. She opened her eyes, accepting her punishment with fatalistic calm. 'Whatever you want.'

'An abortion?'

Pure shock congealed the blood in her veins at the prospect of such a fitting revenge for what she had done to him. '*No*!'

'Not quite *anything*, then.' How could he savage her like this, with such cold mockery, yet hold her so warmly and intimately in his arms? Was this to be her eternal punishment?

'No, not quite anything,' she admitted wearily.

'I told you not to lie to me, Claudia.'

'I'm *trying*!' she cried thickly, tortured by being able to touch him, yet knowing she was not touching him at all.

'Try harder.' With the same grim intensity he asked, 'Do you love me?'

She clenched her teeth, the admission bitter. 'Yes!'

His hand cupped her chin, holding it still for his ruthless interrogation. 'Do you imagine that I love you?'

And aching silence. Not think—*imagine* ... A cruel distinction. What was the truth here and what was the lie? She looked at him, filling her heart and mind and senses with his essence.

'Yes,' she said huskily. 'Otherwise you wouldn't have let me goad you into seeing me again. But that doesn't mean I'll take advantage of it——'

A fugitive gleam of laughter darted like summer lightning across his eyes. 'I can see that you believe that right now, Duchess, but I have no doubt that's going to turn out to be another bold-faced lie. You'll take shameless advantage of my every weakness——'

'Loving isn't a weakness, Morgan,' she protested earnestly, trembling with exquisite relief. 'It makes you strong.'

'Strong enough to conquer the black demons of doubt,' he agreed, smoothing his hand across her sun-warmed bare back. 'Even when I hated you, Claudia, I never doubted that you were mine to hate——'

'Morgan——'

'No, let me say this, so there can be no misunder-standing, so that we can put it behind us.' His finger touched her lower lip, slightly swollen where she had bitten it and drawn blood. 'I would very much like for you to be pregnant with my baby, but, whether you're pregnant or not, I still want to marry you. I chased you, I caught you; I won't give you up easily. We can't change the mistakes of the past but we can definitely shape a better future for ourselves, if both of us are willing. In the last few days I worked out that there was quite a bit of injured pride keeping my angry feelings of betrayal on the boil. I've spent the last few days drunk and thinking ugly thoughts, sulking because life wasn't fair, but then who said it ever was?

'This morning I started to function in the real, unfair world again. And in the real world I found that I still had the same choice I had before I picked up that medical file: life with Claudia and life without Claudia. The same choice... and the same Claudia.

'I know you quite well, you see, and one of your flaws is an annoying habit of protecting yourself from un-pleasantness by ignoring it—like pretending to be tough and mercenary and blasé about sex when you're really a die-hard romantic who would no more fall into bed with a man she didn't love than hurt him if she did.' He lowered his mouth towards hers and his tongue briefly touched the tiny, throbbing wound in a gesture of ex-quisite gentleness.

'You didn't want to hurt Nash so you agreed to marry him although you had doubts; you didn't want to hurt Mark, so you didn't tell him how I insulted you; you didn't want to hurt me so you tried to protect me as long as possible from a knowledge that would, you suspected, cause me more pain than it alleviated——'

'I truly am sorry, Morgan——'

'I know. So am I. For the time we've wasted. You probably would have allowed yourself to be seduced by me a great deal sooner if you hadn't had a guilty secret to protect,' he murmured, enjoying her blush, and the tentative reblooming of her feminine confidence at the casual acceptance implicit in his teasing. 'When I got served those damned papers I lost my temper and nearly punched out those guys, until I realised that you *couldn't* be serious . . . not my passionately soft-hearted Claudia. You were telling me that you hadn't run away. That you were still there for me if I wanted you. *If*?'

His forehead rested against hers, moving back and forth to smooth away the last ruffles as he kissed her nose. 'Whatever wrongs you've done, you taught me a very valuable and necessary lesson two years ago: that life is fragile and every moment we are given is precious to us and to the people who love us. It's due to you that I rediscovered myself and my son . . . and my capacity for love.

'I love you, my darling Duchess, and that's a cause for celebration, never apology. So marry me, and let's enjoy our lifetime of precious moments together. I promise you that I'll make you feel so well-loved that you'll forget there was ever anything but trust between us . . .'

She was feeling beautifully well-loved already, his mouth cherishing hers, his hands moving skilfully under the thin fabric of her maillot, reviving her spirit and coaxing her heart and body into his caressing care.

Their celebration was personal and private but it did indeed have a very lasting and notably public effect.

Nine months later, almost to the very day, little Sarah Stone was delivered upon an unsuspecting world in the awkward confines of a classic Corvette parked crookedly outside a Wellington hospital, her tiny, enraged cry announcing that she had her panic-stricken father's temper and her embarrassed mother's talent for attracting his attention!

Next Month's Romances

Each month you can choose from a wide variety of romance with Mills & Boon. Below are the new titles to look out for next month, why not ask either Mills & Boon Reader Service or your Newsagent to reserve you a copy of the titles you want to buy – just tick the titles you would like and either post to Reader Service or take it to any Newsagent and ask them to order your books.

Please save me the following titles: **Please tick**   ✓

Title	Author	
HEART OF THE OUTBACK	Emma Darcy	
DARK FIRE	Robyn Donald	
SEPARATE ROOMS	Diana Hamilton	
GUILTY LOVE	Charlotte Lamb	
GAMBLE ON PASSION	Jacqueline Baird	
LAIR OF THE DRAGON	Catherine George	
SCENT OF BETRAYAL	Kathryn Ross	
A LOVE UNTAMED	Karen van der Zee	
TRIUMPH OF THE DAWN	Sophie Weston	
THE DARK EDGE OF LOVE	Sara Wood	
A PERFECT ARRANGEMENT	Kay Gregory	
RELUCTANT ENCHANTRESS	Lucy Keane	
DEVIL'S QUEST	Joanna Neil	
UNWILLING SURRENDER	Cathy Williams	
ALMOST AN ANGEL	Debbie Macomber	
THE MARRIAGE BRACELET	Rebecca Winters	

If you would like to order these books in addition to your regular subscription from Mills & Boon Reader Service please send £1.90 per title to: Mills & Boon Reader Service, Freepost, P.O. Box 236, Croydon, Surrey, CR9 9EL, quote your Subscriber No:................................. (If applicable) and complete the name and address details below. Alternatively, these books are available from many local Newsagents including W.H.Smith, J.Menzies, Martins and other paperback stockists from 12 March 1994.

Name:...

Address:...

....Post Code:.......................

To Retailer: If you would like to stock M&B books please contact your regular book/magazine wholesaler for details.

You may be mailed with offers from other reputable companies as a result of this application. If you would rather not take advantage of these opportunities please tick box ☐

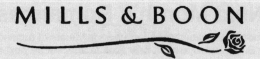

MILLS & BOON

Forthcoming Titles

DUET
Available in February

The Carole Mortimer Duet **ELUSIVE AS THE UNICORN**
MEMORIES OF THE PAST

The Susan Napier Duet **TRUE ENCHANTER**
FORTUNE'S MISTRESS

FAVOURITES
Available in March

A BITTER HOMECOMING Robyn Donald
DARK PURSUIT Charlotte Lamb

LOVE ON CALL
Available in March

NO MORE SECRETS Lilian Darcy
TILL SUMMER ENDS Hazel Fisher
TAKE A DEEP BREATH Margaret O'Neill
HEALING LOVE Meredith Webber

HEARTS OF FIRE

By Miranda Lee

HEARTS OF FIRE by Miranda Lee is a totally compelling six-part saga set in Australia's glamorous but cut-throat world of gem dealing.

Discover the passion, scandal, sin and finally the hope that exist between two fabulously rich families. You'll be hooked from the very first page as Gemma Smith fights for the secret of the priceless **Heart of Fire** black opal and fights for love too...

Each novel features a gripping romance in itself. And **SEDUCTION AND SACRIFICE,** the first title in this exciting series, is due for publication in April but you can order your FREE copy, worth £2.50, NOW! To receive your FREE book simply complete the coupon below and return it to:

**MILLS & BOON READER SERVICE, FREEPOST,
P.O. BOX 236, CROYDON CR9 9EL.   TEL: 081-684 2141**

NO STAMP NEEDED

Ms/Mrs/Miss/Mr: _____   HOF

Address _____

_____

_____

Postcode _____

mps *MAILING PREFERENCE SERVICE*